To Lizzie

Orion's Circle

Sirius Wolves Book one

Victoria Sue

Copyright © 2015 by Victoria Sue

All rights reserved.

No portion of this book may be reproduced in any form without written permission from the publisher or author, except as permitted by U.S. copyright law.

Contents

1. Chapter One — 1
2. Chapter Two — 9
3. Chapter Three — 16
4. Chapter Four — 26
5. Chapter Five — 36
6. Chapter Six — 44
7. Chapter Seven — 57
8. Chapter Eight — 69
9. Chapter Nine — 83
10. Chapter Ten — 90
11. Chapter Eleven — 99
12. Chapter Twelve — 106
13. Chapter Thirteen — 114
14. Chapter Fourteen — 125
15. Chapter Fifteen — 132
16. Chapter Sixteen — 141
17. Chapter Seventeen — 150
18. Chapter Eighteen — 154

19. Epilogue   162

Also By   170

Chapter One

A DEN WAS RUNNING FOR his life. The howls and snarls from the pack reverberated off the trees. Lungs bursting, heart pumping, and legs shaking he careered on desperately, losing count of the number of times he fell and pushed to his feet. The gammas who were chasing him were getting nearer. His skin crawled with trails of blood from where the branches had cut his body, and he cried out in pain as his bare foot caught on some creepers and catapulted him headlong to the ground. Exhaustion shook his arms as he tried to push himself up, but a bolt of agony through his ankle kept him on the floor. Dizziness, pain, and hopelessness swirled around him.

He hung his tired head. He was done, he simply couldn't fight anymore. Months of imprisonment, starvation, and torture for the Alpha's amusement had all led to this moment—the Ceremonial Hunt to mark the acceptance of a new Alpha was to the death—*his death*. His thin, bare shoulders shook as he heard the wolves surround him, but it was the overpowering hatred that assaulted him. Hatred—in every look, in every word, and finally in every punch.

He lifted his eyes heavenwards, half searching, but it was futile. He didn't believe in any super beings—the enchanted that had been whispered about by his grandparents—Sirius's magical wolves that would bring about the order that mankind needed, the balance. There was no mythical being to save Aden. He would be dead before Sirius ascended, and as he peered to the east, he knew it wouldn't be long until the earth's brightest star shone.

As the wolves circled and brought with them their familiar stench, Aden's head echoed with his mother's entreaties to run and his father's pleas to the Alpha to spare him. It had done no good, and if he'd known their blood would have been sacrificed to mark the start of the hunt, he would have done his best to stop them saying anything. At least he would have been spared the sight of the Alpha and his gammas ripping their flesh as they were butchered.

"That's right," the booming voice of the old Alpha sounded. "Cower like the filth that you are. You're completely useless, boy. We've had no sport at all." He'd clearly shifted back, and by the sniggers and taunts so had some of the pack. Aden hung his head; he knew better than to attempt to reason.

"I think that would depend on your definition of sport."

The forest suddenly went silent at the new voice. Aden gazed upwards towards the speaker, a man, his voice practically vibrating with anger. The hair on Aden's arms prickled with the fury that swept around the clearing, and while Aden had cowered at the sound of the Alpha's voice, this one sent chills through his body as each word resonated through the forest. Aden zeroed in on the huge man leaning casually on a tree. His jet black hair fell over his smooth, tanned face, and he was huge, at least six foot five—hell the man's body was nearly the width of the tree trunk he leaned against, his shirt material straining against his biceps as he casually crossed his arms. He was clothed, that in itself a crushing disappointment as his clothing marked him as obviously human—and the man didn't smell like a shifter. All Aden's pack smelled like the Alpha—musty, like something was decaying. *Their humanity*, Aden thought, feeling helpless.

All the shifters including himself were naked. Whatever clothes they were wearing either discarded or destroyed as the hunt started and they shifted. Aden was naked because that's how he had been imprisoned. He hadn't been allowed clothes for such a long time. For one second…Aden shook his head, angry that the man had given him a tiny kernel of hope, only to be crushed. He was clearly a powerful man, but no man was a match for any wolf shifter, never mind a whole pack. He would be ripped apart, and Aden had had enough of people being slaughtered because of him that day. He had to try and distract the wolves so they would let the human go.

Aden tried not to wince as he managed to get up. He focused away from the constant pain that made him feel sick—as if he had any food in his stomach to make him so. He didn't think he had been fed for at least two days, and the ever present hunger made it very hard to mark the passing of time.

"Alpha Richard," he said, "ignore the man, he doesn't understand. I will try again and will be better sport this time."

Aden ignored howls of laughter that surrounded him. Wolves were supposed to be better than humans. He'd been taught their superior strength and speed was a gift of the gods, and just because the others chose to ignore the old teachings didn't mean he had to. No one else was going to die today because of him. The human pushed himself away from the tree.

"Sport?" The stranger spat the word with contempt.

Aden almost shook his head. The stupid man was digging his own grave. Humans had known about wolf shifters for years, had even tried to contain the packs in smaller designated areas, ignoring traditional pack land boundaries. When that hadn't worked humans and wolves had chosen to ignore each other, their existence buried with each passing century, but just because Aden had been taught to mistrust humans for years didn't mean he wanted to see one of them die.

Aden glanced at the man. He had to try and get him out of trouble, try to keep him alive. Maybe Sirius was looking down and had deemed Aden's suffering would come to an end, maybe—just maybe—this was a test. That's what his grandfather would have said. He had to try. "This isn't your business," Aden said. "For your own safety you must leave."

The large man swung around and his bright blue eyes burned into Aden. "Don't be frightened, little one. Your desire to protect does you credit." Aden blinked as a feeling of calmness washed over him. It was unreal. He wasn't even sure he was afraid anymore. The man looked almost fondly at him, and then turned to Alpha Richard. "This isn't sport. How can a smaller wolf—a submissive wolf—go against a whole pack?"

Aden just had time to wonder why the guy knew what a submissive wolf was, and how he knew that Aden was one, when snarls started again, as at the Alpha's nod the gammas closest to the Alpha shifted back. The large man smiled. To Aden, he looked almost *pleased* at the Alpha's reaction, which was impossible. Alpha Richard threw his head back and laughed in contempt, and the man just tutted. "Alpha Richard, this is your last warning. Stand down."

To be fair to the old Alpha, he did look shocked that the stranger knew his name. Then he blustered, deciding to ignore the fact that the man knew they were wolves. "I have no quarrel with you. Be gone, stranger. This is wolf business."

"Exactly." The word was no sooner uttered by the stranger when everyone heard the rustling behind him and two of the biggest wolves Aden had ever seen calmly padded out of the trees and stood on either side of the stranger. One was golden brown, and the other was simply breathtaking—the coat looked pure silver. Aden had never seen a shifter that color.

The closest golden brown one immediately pricked his ears up and fixed his gaze on Aden. Before Aden had the chance to wonder if this was a new threat, and yet something else that wanted to kill him, the wolf put its head back and howled. Aden shivered and his pack immediately backed away slightly at the noise. The howl wasn't something most of their wolves did anymore, at least not like that, the howls from his pack were almost scratchy as if they had lost their power. This echo was a statement. A challenge.

The blue eyed stranger looked as startled as Aden, and quickly turned to Aden as if appraising him. Then, before Aden could even think to panic, the golden wolf calmly trotted up to him and rubbed his flank along Aden's legs. Aden stumbled at the weight, his arms flailing slightly since he didn't have anything to grab a hold of. Quick as a flash the wolf had bent around him and pushed his head up into Aden's other hand to steady him. Aden didn't question it, he just grabbed a hold of the thick coat and tried to concentrate on locking his knees together. He barely had a chance to register the fresh, clean scent of lemons. The stranger nodded as if in agreement with the brown wolf, and turned to the Alpha.

"Be gone, Alpha, and take your miserable pack with you. The gammas from Jefferson have already been summoned to monitor your pack lands. I am not pleased with what I have witnessed here today." The man suddenly pushed away from the tree, muscles rippling, and advanced towards the Alpha.

"W-what?" The Alpha, shocked, took two steps backwards and nearly stumbled. Then he seemed to recover and Aden's heart sank as he registered the look in the Alpha's eyes that he had seen countless times before. It wasn't determination; it was cruelty, cruelty and glee. Richard smiled, and Aden tensed, wanting to shout a warning.

With a flicker of Richard's eyes the gammas bunched their hind legs and prepared to launch at the stranger. If Aden had blinked he would have missed it.

Just as the gammas pounced, a silver flash of fur swept in front of him and the strong smell of blood rose in the air. Five gammas lay dead with their throats torn out. Aden blinked, horrified, and swallowed down sudden nausea. The silver wolf sat and casually licked the blood off its paws.

"Do you want to try that again?"

Alpha Richard goggled at the stranger, awestruck. The gammas that were left alive whimpered and slunk back. Aden's heart was hammering so loud he swore all the others could hear it.

Entranced, Aden stared at the wolf. Its long tongue wrapped around each paw, slowly, sensuously. Each swipe sent shivers down Aden's spine. Such focus, such...Aden shook his head to clear it. It was mesmerizing. The silver wolf paused and cocked its head at Aden. He barely had time to blink before another massive, fury body entwined itself around Aden's legs. The silver wolf paused as its nose bumped with the golden one, seemed to consider Aden, then pushed its head under Aden's other hand.

Aden cried out at the sudden explosion of pain in his wrist. He closed his eyes and bit his lip furiously. His wrist had been crushed yesterday when the Alpha had grabbed him, but with everything else that hurt, a wrist wasn't so important. He opened his eyes as he felt the silver wolf cautiously sniff his fingers, then slowly a pink tongue licked the tip of his finger.

Heat bathed Aden's hand and the pain trickled out of his fingers until it was gone. Aden blinked, his sluggish brain trying to catch up. How had the wolf done that? He stared into mesmerizing gray eyes, so calm. Aden took a slow breath, and dug his fingers in as the wolf's silver head butted his hand again.

Alpha Richard was stammering at this point. "I-I have no quarrel with visiting shifters on my land." If Aden had the strength, he would have laughed. *No quarrel?* The Alpha would have ripped them limb from limb. Everyone knew they were forbidden to have contacts with any other pack.

He must have made some noise, because Alpha Richard looked at Aden. "Come," the Alpha said furiously.

Aden's heart jumped, then constricted. He felt the Alpha power swirling around him with the order, warring with the misery he knew it would bring. He was helpless to disobey and knew the punishment he would receive for the hunt being spoiled would make him wish the strangers had never interrupted his death. At least it would be over now. It was his susceptibility to Richard's power that marked him as an omega, everyone said so. Unconsciously he tightened his grip in the golden wolf's fur, and felt the huge animal lean closer.

"I don't think so." The stranger added determinedly. "The omega stays with us."

"Aden, come here." The Alpha completely ignored the man and pushed a little too hard. Defenseless, Aden let go of the wolf and raised his hands to his head to stave off the pain. He felt battered. Stumbling, he sank to his knees. He didn't have the pride to keep him upright anymore. His body was worn down, beaten and starved for so many weeks while he was held captive for amusement.

His parents had managed to keep him out of sight for so long when he hadn't shifted at fifteen like all the other wolves. It had been a stupid game of tag with the younger cubs he had been minding all those months ago that had sealed his fate. Jay, his best friend, had chased after him, and he'd run, only realizing he'd wandered onto the Alpha's personal grounds when the gammas surrounded them all and had commanded they shift and pledge obedience. One by one his friends had shifted and lay prone in the favored position of obedience shown to the Alpha. Until it was Aden's turn. And of course, he couldn't. Aden had been thrown into the small cage in the corner of the Alpha's hallway, after being stripped naked and beaten until he lost consciousness. Then that became an almost daily occurrence, and it had been worse today because of the hunt. He'd wished for so much in those first few months, wished that he hadn't been cursed as an omega, wished that despite his inability to shift he still didn't have the recovery of a shifter body, because while his injuries wouldn't heal totally, it healed him enough so they didn't kill him. Then, finally, when he gave up on being rescued, he simply wished for his own death.

The hunt? It was pitiful. Starvation was making him lightheaded, but the hours he spent in the cage atrophied his muscles to the point where walking was painful. How he had managed to run at all amazed him. No, he thought bitterly, that wasn't why he was so amazed. It was why he'd bothered to run at all that defied belief, because it was futile. He'd thought today was finally his day to die anyway. Defeated, he struggled to his feet for what he hoped would be the last time.

He must have made some small whimper of protest, since the stranger swung his gaze away from the Alpha and back to him. In the distance, Aden heard Richard snarl and take a step towards him, but he didn't have a chance to be afraid as an enormous black wolf appeared from nowhere and struck—once, deadly. Even the birds overhead didn't screech to interrupt the shocked silence. It was as if the very forest held its breath as Richard's head rolled away from his body, his unseeing eyes staring heavenward, a fat pink tongue extending from his mouth, following the gasp he made as his life ended. The stench was incredible, as if the Alpha had died and rotted before he ever lost his life. Aden barely was aware of two of the younger gammas still in human form, turning and losing whatever they had eaten that day.

As the black wolf turned back to face him, Aden shook his head in confusion at what he was seeing, and he swayed. The same brilliant blue eyes of the large stranger were staring at him, but not in a human body. The huge black, Alpha-marked body of the biggest wolf Aden had ever seen took a step towards him. He watched, almost fascinated, wondering if now was the time he would die.

Do not fear me, little one. No one will ever hurt you again.

Aden stared, confused, into two brilliant blue eyes, kind eyes. His last thought as he gave up his fight to stay conscious was whether or not the strong arms that gently caught him would keep a tight hold on him forever.

Chapter Two

A DEN BLINKED AWAKE AS the most amazing smell hit him. Like pure snow in a pine forest, clean and sharp.

"I think that woke him up, Alpha." Aden opened his eyes, saw the dark-haired stranger from the forest smiling at him, turned to the voice that spoke softly by his ear, and was met by the sight of another beautiful human being. But where the first stranger had been dark, this man was fair. His blond hair flopped casually over tanned skin and warm brown eyes. Aden blinked at the smell—*lemons*—and moved closer without any conscious thought. The first stranger he had seen in the woods walked fully into the room.

The fair-haired man next to him chuckled. "Do I have to?" He smiled softly at Aden. Aden's lips curved in answer, and as the man set the tray down, he almost wept as his stomach growled, the delicious scent of bacon and sausages meeting his nose.

"Yes, Alpha." The fair-haired wolf bobbed his head, and climbed out. Aden was just trying to understand the odd one way conversation, when his throat completely dried up. The guy had got out of bed completely naked, and reached to the chair for his pants. Aden stared shamelessly at the rippling muscles that bunched and fell and fairly danced across the golden skin on his smooth back.

He turned, put his head on one side, and extended his arm to cup Aden's face. Aden was suddenly assaulted with a desperate need to lean into the man's hand. It felt so warm, so right, as if he belonged just there. Aden's eyes drifted closed as he bathed in the feeling of safety it gave him, and the soft scent of lemons still present. The bed bounced lightly, and the first guy sat down. They both looked at each other and the second man dropped his hand. Aden couldn't help a small sound of protest.

Without looking at him, the first man nodded at the second. "Join Darric, Conner. I must speak to the omega first."

Aden watched the man—Conner—walk away, and was immediately swamped with distress. He moved restlessly. No, he didn't want him to go.

"Pl—" Aden bit down furiously on the begging words, and ridiculous tears threatened to roll down his face—ridiculous because he had stopped crying weeks ago, all his tears had been beaten out of him. He must have made a small choking sound because the man immediately frowned.

"I'm sorry, little one. I forget you will feel the loss more acutely until the bond has been formed." Aden closed his eyes on the burning, and despaired at the desolation he was surrounded with. He sank further into his own misery, convinced this was an elaborate trick of the mind. How could he feel so strongly about someone he had met barely seconds ago? He had probably been dreaming, his beating so bad this time he had finally lost his mind.

"You are as sane as me," the stranger said slowly, and moved towards him on the bed. Aden opened his eyes as the man held his arms out. "Come here."

Aden didn't hesitate, not once. His brain registered the immense feeling of power emanating from the man, but where it should have caused him distress and pain—as it did with Alpha Richard—he was just desperate to get as near to the stranger as humanly possible. He nearly sobbed in relief as he was drawn into strong arms and wrapped up protectively. This felt so right, so perfect, and whatever this insanity he had descended into, he would revel in it for however long he was granted. Aden closed his eyes, and released a happy sigh.

"Shh..." He heard a chuckle and felt the man's chest rumble as he was pulled against it.

Aden inhaled the man's scent once more, and it sent tingles of sensation down his body. He hardly dared open his eyes for fear the feeling would go. If someone had told him he had been given drugs he would have believed them, believed them and asked for more.

"It's natural. Your wolf recognizes its mate."

Aden's eyes shot open at the outrageous statement. As omega it had been drilled into him painfully that he would never mate. His lot was to take on the suffering of the pack, simply stated, his suffering was for the greater good. There was no part of that suffering that involved him having the comfort of a mate. Besides which, he couldn't shift so he didn't have a wolf.

"Who told you all those ridiculous lies?"

The stranger tipped his head at him; Aden didn't realize he had just spoken out loud.

"I'm dead aren't I? Or insane?" Aden persisted.

He felt the man's smile as his lips brushed against his hair. "No. I need you to eat, try and get your strength back. I have much to explain—" The man tipped Aden's face back gently. "But for now, please eat."

Aden shook his head in total disbelief, but eyed the plate longingly.

Maybe this was an elaborate trick and the food was poisoned? The man reached out and snagged a piece of bacon. He pushed it between his lips and crunched.

"Safe, see? And you will offend Lilly if you don't like her cooking." Aden was astounded. Snatches of memory came back from last night. This man, whoever he was, seemed to know what Aden was thinking; Aden hadn't said out loud the food may be poisoned.

"I do. I know what all my mates think. And, I'm sorry, my name is Blaze. I should have told you that already. Eat, it isn't poisoned. I need you well, and happy." Blaze ran a finger down Aden's face again, and before Aden could even respond to the astounding feeling of being called someone's mate, he was struck with a sense of peace. Peace and security. He leaned further into the big chest that was supporting him, and smiled when he felt it rumble in response. Blaze reached a large hand out and snagged a piece of bacon, but instead of eating it, he brought it to Aden's lips. Aden opened his mouth automatically, and crunched down on the best tasting food that had passed his lips in so very long.

He shivered at the memory of being force fed the slop they had given him, when he had tried to refuse. Eventually he'd hoped starvation would bring him death, but they had always seemed to know how much to give him to barely keep him alive. He turned his face away slightly, stomach protesting, at the fourth piece. The hand dropped. "You have been starved for a long time, little one. You will eat small amounts regularly until you adapt to being able to take full meals."

"Aden. My name's Aden." Not that Aden minded really what Blaze called him when he was being treated so well, but "little one" made him feel like a child.

"Aden, of course." Blaze laid him back against the soft pillows. "I will try and remember, but compared to me, you are little. It's not an insult."

Blaze was still smiling as he said it, but Aden had a hard time concentrating on him. He was getting sleepy again, but he also really needed to go to the bathroom.

"Come on then, I will help."

Aden blushed furiously. *There was no way.* Then he remembered Blaze could hear his thoughts and tried to look apologetic. He stared, fascinated, as Blaze's big-bellied laugh resounded in the room.

Blaze helped him to sit near the edge of the enormous bed that was wide enough for nearly all his old pack to climb in. "I will help you get there, then leave you to your privacy." Blaze cupped Aden's chin again, and he raised his eyes. "I will only leave you if I am satisfied you will not hurt yourself."

He brushed a thumb over Aden's cheek. "You are mine to protect, little—*Aden.*"

Aden smiled in gratitude at his name, and shuffled to his feet. He must have stood too quickly, as giddiness nearly had him on the floor, and Blaze held him steadily. Aden raised confused eyes, and wriggled his fingers. He hadn't just dreamt that the silver wolf healed him—he suddenly realized his ribs no longer hurt either.

"You are healed, but not even Darric can reverse your body's mistreatment so quickly."

"He can heal? He healed *me*?" Aden almost gaped in astonishment. That was one powerful gift. There had been whispers in the pack about shifters that had such power, and some wolves that could heal just by shifting, but most thought them old wives' tales now.

Blaze frowned. "Your pack is unable to heal by shifting?"

Aden looked confused. "Yours can?"

Blaze sighed and gazed at Aden with troubled eyes. "I think I have been very remiss in not taking a closer look at your pack before. We have been establishing larger ties with the help of Jefferson pack." A warm thumb grazed his cheek, and Blaze smiled slightly. "But enough for now, we must get you well first."

"We?"

"Lean on me, get your bearings." Aden did gratefully, even knowing Blaze had completely ignored his question, and managed to get to the bathroom. He'd heard of Jefferson pack before. Alpha Richard had banned all their wolves from having any sort of interaction with them for conspiring with humans. Aden hadn't really taken much notice of the order to be honest, it wasn't like he would ever get to meet any of them. Blaze helped him lower a soft pair of shorts down he hadn't realized he was wearing, and sat him down. Blaze gave him a careful look, and disappeared outside the door.

Aden relieved himself with a sigh, and gripped the seat, determined to stand to wash his hands. He never got the chance as Blaze reappeared almost clucking in annoyance at his small attempt at independence. If Aden was honest with himself, he would have never made it to the sink and then back to bed without Blaze.

"Come here." Not that Blaze gave him any choice, as he sat him down on the bed and pulled him closer. "Thirsty?" He held out a glass of milk, and Aden tried not to be totally embarrassed as he guzzled it in delight.

"Did your pack have any interaction with the other local packs? Jefferson? White Waters?"

Aden shook his head when the milk was finished. "We were told not to." He thought hard. "To be honest, I've never heard of White Waters, but Alpha Richard always said our pack was stronger than Jefferson." Aden didn't bother saying Jefferson was conspiring with humans, he knew Blaze would have heard his thoughts.

Blaze smiled knowingly. "Jefferson pack has over thirteen hundred wolves. Their pack lands stretch for thousands of miles from Fort Collins to

Canon City, and as far west as Glenwood Springs."

Aden gaped, he'd only vaguely heard of Fort Collins. "But we had only around three hundred wolves."

"Which is exactly why we haven't bothered your pack yet. Hunter told us your pack, Black Lakes, was very old fashioned, and...closeted."

Aden stared at Blaze. He knew what he was saying. "You mean all packs aren't like that...and who's Hunter?"

"Hunter is the Alpha of Jefferson."

"You don't belong to Jefferson pack." Aden frowned, confused. "You have your own pack, then?"

Blaze settled down further and pulled Aden in comfortably. "Were you ever told about the legend of Sirius?"

"Vaguely, I think by my grandma." Aden tried to keep up with the odd conversation, trying to decide if Blaze was deliberately not answering him. "The older wolves used to say Sirius sent a wolf shifter to save mankind. I can't remember much else though."

Blaze frowned. "I hadn't realized so much of our history was being lost, although I think your old pack is maybe one of the worse I have come across in a while."

Aden looked at Blaze and suddenly wondered how old he was. He took a breath to start asking questions when there was a knock at the door, and a smaller man with gray hair put his head around the door.

"My apologies Alpha, you're needed. There is a delegation from the Black Lakes pack inquiring after their omega. One of them is being—"

Aden gasped and the man stopped speaking. He looked apologetic, but Aden took little notice.

They had come for him. He knew this wasn't real, it wouldn't last. Tears burned in his eyes and the old familiar misery crept over him. This was it then. He had enjoyed a fantasy for an hour. He buried his head and counted the seconds until it would be ripped away.

Chapter Three

"Aden." He ignored Blaze's voice as panic set in.

"Aden," repeated Blaze when he got no response. Aden lifted miserable eyes.

Blaze smiled and pulled him nearer. He brushed a kiss over Aden's head and Aden looked up in shock. He stood up and Aden felt the same desperate sense of loss as he had before when Conner had left. "I think," Blaze said, bending down, "it will be better if you hear this too." Aden gasped as he felt himself swung up into Blaze's arms. "Besides which, it will make you sick to be parted from us all. Rest your head. You are not strong enough yet."

Aden was more than happy to *rest his head*. In fact, anything that involved him burrowing in that amazing fresh scent was fine by him. That and the fact he was sure his face was probably crimson as Blaze marched out of the room carrying him. In between the milk, his nickname, and the fact that he doubted he would be able to walk anywhere near as fast as Blaze, he felt about seven years old.

Aden smiled into the chest as he felt it rumbling in amusement. He felt Blaze's arms tighten a little as he walked into another room, and didn't really want to look. He could smell the rancid odor surrounding his pack, and he buried his nose again.

Low growls sounded around the room; another voice spoke up, low and powerful. "How dare you come here and think to threaten us?"

Aden immediately lifted his head at the other voice. He quivered, and didn't understand why. It wasn't fear exactly, more a recognition of...he didn't know, but whoever had spoken was out of sight, and he strained his neck to see around the crowded room. It looked like half his pack had turned up. He moved out of Blaze's embrace. "Let me down, I can stand." He took a step forward and tilted his head to see the man who had spoken earlier. Aden stumbled in shock, as the most beautiful man Aden had ever seen turned to look at him. Aden's eyes were riveted to the smile that spread slowly on the man's gorgeous face, the smooth ebony skin with high cheekbones, and the nearly silver hair. It was a stunning combination, making Aden gulp.

More growls sounded and Aden glanced at the wolves from Black Lakes. He cringed. He loved being held after being denied any kind human touch for so long, but he really had to man up. Aden tilted his chin higher and he took a step away from Blaze as he turned to face his pack. He felt the emotions bounce around the room, and coalesce into him as usual. He stood straighter. This was what he did, even though it was painful; an omega, he was always told, absorbed all negative emotions and diffused them. He'd just never been able to be good enough at it for Alpha Richard, and taking his hatred had hurt him most of all.

He surveyed the men in front of him. Bayer, the Alpha's old beta, and his two sons. The gammas that had survived yesterday. He was surprised to see Kellan—he didn't know he was being trained as a gamma. Jay, Aden's best friend, was Kellan's younger brother, but Kellan had his blond head firmly lowered and wouldn't look at Aden. A few of the young men looked downright terrified, and he was grateful that Jay wasn't here to witness this.

Two men moved and Aden's breath caught as his gaze landed on the green eyes staring from the pock marked face of the man Aden hated the most.

Gregory Madden, Alpha Richard's personal physician. He tried to swallow, but his throat felt stuck. This man had made every punishment ten times worse, and it wasn't even the pain, it was the sick sound of bones popping as he put them back. Blackness edged Aden's sight as the simpering voice he'd heard nearly every morning echoed in his head. *Have to make sure they don't heal crooked.* That was what Madden had said every time, but the bastard had always made the healing worse than the injury in the first place.

Snarls penetrated Aden's thoughts at the same time as he was wrapped up in strong arms. Aden blinked the panic away, and inhaled slowly. Lemons…it was Conner that held him, and he breathed deeply. He was safe, safe for now anyway.

Safe for always.

Aden raised grateful eyes to Blaze. He knew it was him that had spoken. He shook the thoughts away as another snarl from Conner stole his breath.

"You look well, omega." Gregory Madden casually pushed to the front, and Aden backed further into Conner. That's what he used to say every morning. Then he would laugh, as the Alpha planned all that was guaranteed to make Aden unwell. Aden shivered as the green eyes lit with assessment, and memories plucked from nightmares slithered up his skin.

The arms around him shook slightly, pulling Aden into the present. Another tremble worked its way through those arms and Aden looked up concerned, then stunned, as he took in Conner's face.

Conner's furious gaze pinned the doctor. The hand that wasn't curled around Aden was fisted and shaking. Conner's whole body was shaking and Aden could tell he was barely controlling himself. A sheen of gold fur had sprouted along Conner's arms, and his soft brown eyes glinted amber.

Without thinking or even registering that Conner could also hear his thoughts, Aden lifted his hand to Conner's face and pulled it down to him.

The big man was shaking because he was holding in check his need to shift. *You don't have to do this. I'm safe.*

The effect was immediate, and Aden was stunned as the tension bled out of Conner's face and the stiff hold of his shoulders loosened. Aden braced and waited for the inevitable pain that would accompany taking Conner's anger, but his lips parted in absolute shock when it didn't come. It *always* hurt. How was this time different?

Conner nuzzled Aden's hand. *It's not supposed to hurt. Not from us.* Aden's lips parted in wonder as he heard Conner's voice clearly in his head, then another voice jolted him into the present.

"You stole our omega. We demand return of what is rightfully ours. He is the property of Black Lakes pack." The man that had spoken pushed through between Bayer and Gregory. Aden trembled slightly and pushed back into Conner's chest. It was Craig, the son of Alpha Richard. His Alpha ceremony had been the cause of the hunt. When the current Alpha reached the age of one hundred, either he relinquished to his elder son, or he was challenged. That must mean Craig was Alpha now. That, and the fact his father had had his head ripped off by Blaze.

Craig shot Aden such a look of disgust. Why? Why did everyone hate him so much? Memories of the cage battered him, of Craig laughing and being egged on by his father. The sharp pain of the knife when it was prodded through the bars and there wasn't enough room for him to get away.

Aden felt two large arms surround his shoulders possessively, protectively, and he could have wept with gratitude. His hand itched for the memory of Conner's face, and Conner lightly clasped Aden's wrist, turned it gently palm upwards and softly breathed a kiss onto his skin. It was the gentlest touch Aden had felt in months, and he blinked quickly as his world seemed to still.

Conner gazed at him with his brown eyes and Aden's heart jumped. He'd felt an incredible attraction to both of them from the start, but this? This was stronger, and he was only just beginning to realize that. His mom had always spoken of the second she'd seen his dad. *Perfect mates.* It didn't happen much in his old pack anymore, and Aden had never given that much thought either as he wasn't destined to have one, but...perfect? The look in those brown eyes was so perfect and alive, Aden could nearly reach out and touch it. His breath caught and Conner seemed to shimmer in front of him.

Aden blinked furiously.

"That's disgusting," Craig spat, and took a step forward.

Blaze opened his mouth, but he was beaten to it once more by the silver-haired man. "Be very careful not to insult our mate. Nothing would give me greater pleasure than helping you to meet your father again."

Aden nearly gasped. Mate? Conner had a mate? Aden bit his lip furiously. Well of course he did. Aden tried to step away from Conner but Conner held him tightly.

"Omegas can't have mates," Craig insisted.

Aden wanted to laugh hysterically. Craig had misunderstood, how could anyone think this beautiful man would ever mate someone as pathetic as him?

Craig stood, hands fisted, face reddening. Aden could feel Craig's Alpha power start to throb around the room, and he wanted to weep as he waited for the pain in his mind to increase until he capitulated. Any minute now he would have no choice but to agree.

Conner bent and murmured in his ear. "You have nothing to fear. You don't have to go with them." Aden's lips parted on a word of denial, until a feeling of peace washed over him. He lifted grateful eyes to Blaze, who had moved silently and touched his arm.

With dawning confidence, he turned to face the Alpha.

Craig looked confused, frustrated, and Craig's gammas were murmuring indecisively. They looked equally surprised that Aden wasn't prostrate at their feet.

"This has gone on long enough." Blaze stepped forward and everyone instantly quieted. Blaze fixed his stare on Craig. "You are Alpha of Black Lakes. If you choose to conduct yourself appropriately and run a good pack according to shifter law, you will be allowed to remain. If not, I will choose a new Alpha to lead your wolves."

Craig gaped unattractively at Blaze's words and Aden shared in his astonishment.

"You will allow? Who are you to interfere?" Craig scoffed, and Aden thought if he had been present yesterday when his father had lost his head,

Craig wouldn't have been so sure of himself. Aden heard a quiet laugh behind him, and smiled.

Can you hear everything? Aden asked.

Yes, little one. Aden glanced, startled, at Blaze. He knew he had called him that deliberately so he would know who had spoken to him. He looked at Conner.

Yes, mate.

Aden's eyes rounded, that was definitely Conner that had spoken.

Conner's brown eyes softened into a smile.

Mate? You mean me? Aden stared in complete disbelief.

Of course we mean you. Aden stared at Blaze, astounded. Two? He had two mates? Aden barely had time to register their words as the silver-haired man's voice echoed through his mind.

Three, Aden, three. You have three mates.

Vaguely aware of Conner behind him, the gray eyes speared his gaze. His chest heaved, lungs unable to work, the cogs in his brain no longer able to turn as brakes slammed in surrender. Powerful eyes scanned his body, peeling back every layer, and despite all the times he had spent naked, Aden realized this was the first time in his life he had been truly stripped bare. It was a good job Conner kept a tight hold, because standing on his own was impossible, he wanted to dissolve in a puddle of desperate need at this beautiful man's feet.

He didn't register the other words being spoken by Blaze, he was too busy being aware of every inch of his skin glowing, and his body pulsing. He drew in a shuddering breath, trying to calm his body—a body that hadn't responded favorably to anything in almost a year—and was grateful as Conner's possessive arms wrapped tighter around his abdomen. Steadying him. Grounding him.

Aden blinked as he heard shouting. His old pack were surrounded by Blaze's gammas, and Craig, seeming to be blessed with the same lack of self-preservation as his father, was yelling and protesting as the gammas shoved him out of the room. Blaze ignored them and nodded to Conner. Conner calmly turned Aden around and hoisted him up. The friction on his dick was immediate and Aden groaned and laid his head on Conner's shoulder. He heard a soft laugh behind him from Blaze, and Aden burrowed his head as Conner started walking, convinced his face must be scarlet.

He felt amusement from Conner, and snuggled unashamedly. His dick was being pressed flush against Conner's hard abdomen, brushing a little as Conner walked. Aden reveled in the delicious sensations.

He'd known since he was ten that girls weren't his thing when Alicia Feltman had tried to kiss him in the clearing next to his house. His friends, especially Jay, had whooped and whistled until he'd blushed. What they didn't know was he'd have rather been kissed by Jay's older brother, Kellan. He wasn't stupid though. The Alpha hated gays with a vengeance, spouting about abominations at the monthly pack meeting. When his shift didn't happen and he knew he would be relegated to an omega, fancying boys suddenly became the least of his problems.

Conner deposited Aden on the bed again, and brushed a lock of Aden's too long brown hair out of his eyes.

Little one. Blaze sat on the bed, on the other side of Aden from Conner. "I know you have questions. We were hoping to take this slower for you, but your old pack interrupted that. You still need lots of rest and food."

Aden looked up at Blaze, exasperated. Yes, he was bone tired, but hungry? Not so much. Thanks to his old pack he was used to existing on tiny amounts. He heard a low growl and swung his head to an angry looking Conner. Aden automatically rested his hand on top of Conner's much larger one and felt the man's anger fade.

"Thank you." Conner brushed a kiss on Aden's cheek and Aden's face flushed as immediate heat washed over his body. Conner smirked.

He heard laughter around the room, and wanted to slap his head. "You can all do it, can't you?" he said, half-annoyed. "Read my mind? Know what I'm thinking?"

Blaze nodded solemnly.

"I'm sorry. I will try and guard my thoughts. I—"

"No."

Aden raised startled eyes to the silver-haired giant who bent down to kneel on the floor in front of him. "Please, never shield your thoughts from us. I would feel..."

"Lost." Conner added, and brushed a kiss on the hand that covered his own.

Aden opened his mouth. He couldn't keep calling the guy by the color of his hair. The guy in question put his head back and laughed out loud. Conner snickered too.

"It's Darric, beautiful," the silver-haired man said, trailing his hand down Aden's leg. Aden shivered at the touch and his cock grew hard again, making him blush.

"You have questions?" Blaze took Aden's other hand and Aden smiled at the man that had cared enough to keep him alive yesterday. It was at that point when he gave up protesting at being called little one.

"So, why me? Is it because I am an omega?" As soon as he asked the question, Aden knew it was ridiculous. It wasn't like he was the only omega in existence. There weren't many, but he didn't think for one second these three would have problems with guys lining up to get their hands on them. He frowned. *Or girls. It could just as well be girls.*

Blaze smiled. "To answer both your questions, it's not because you're an omega."

"And it's not girls either," murmured Darric, "but I think you knew that."

"But if it's not because I'm an omega—"

Aden cringed slightly as his voice rose. He could hear the panic weave into his words. If they didn't want him as an omega, he had no other skills. He wasn't even good at being a wolf, he couldn't even shift for pity's sake. He sucked at that too.

Blaze immediately cupped his face. Conner leaned in closer, and Darric clasped his leg. Before Aden had chance to marvel at the show of comfort from all three of them, Blaze was speaking again.

"You aren't actually an omega, and you were never made to shift."

Aden looked at Blaze in astonishment. "But, they—he, Alpha Richard—they all said I was. That's why I could take on their suffering, why it was my job." Aden lowered his voice. "Why I will never get a mate, because all my emotion belongs to the pack. To take their suffering because I'm no good at anything else."

Conner growled low in his throat. Aden squeezed his hand automatically. Blaze stood up and paced.

Quick as a flash, Darric sat down next to Aden. Aden could feel the desire coming off the man like a battering ram. Aden wanted to pant. He couldn't believe he would ever be the focus of such emotion.

"Darric." Blaze growled the name out in warning. Darric glanced at Blaze apologetically and Aden felt some of the desire dissipate a little. Aden breathed a little easier.

"I've always been told homosexuality is a disease," Aden said. "I thought that's why my wolf had deserted me. Why I would never shift, and that made me an omega." Aden bit his lip to stop it wobbling slightly.

Blaze looked softly at Aden. "Do we look sick to you? And your wolf is there in spirit, he is what gives your body its shifter strength. You just need to reconnect with him. But no, you will never shift. You are not supposed to. Your greatest achievement is your human body, and your abilities only manifest themselves in that form."

Aden looked at what was possibly the best three specimens of manhood he had ever seen. They were even more beautiful than Jay, and he had girls falling over him all the time.

"Who's Jay?" Darric nearly growled the question out, and Aden wanted to laugh with delight.

Then Blaze's words finally got his attention. "What do you mean I'm not an omega?"

Blaze paused in his pacing. "Little one, you have been mistaken for an omega by wolves too selfish and too ignorant to know your true worth."

"If they knew…" Conner shuddered.

Alarm skittered along his spine. "What do you mean?"

"You are Psi." Darric laid his head on Aden's shoulder.

"Psi? What?" Aden was really confused. He had no clue what this Psi was.

"Psi completes Orion's Circle," Blaze answered solemnly as if that explained everything.

Aden shook his head. Between the emotions rolling off Darric and the comfort he was giving to Conner, his head was spinning with confusion.

Blaze cocked his head to one side. "Leave us."

Aden had a second to realize Blaze wasn't talking to him when Conner and Darric smiled and rose. They both looked longingly at Aden, then turned and left the room.

Aden barely had a chance to miss their presence when Blaze started talking. He reached out a hand to Aden. "Come, sit with me. I have to explain how Orion's Circle will help to save mankind."

Chapter Four

BLAZE STUDIED ADEN, WHO shut his gaping mouth with a snap. "Come, sit with me?" Blaze asked again.

Aden followed Blaze to the chairs in the corner of the large room arranged next to the window. Aden headed for the chair beside Blaze, but was stopped by him and pulled into his lap. Aden breathed a sigh and cuddled shamelessly, despite his mind whirling, feeling contentment creeping over him.

Blaze took a breath. "Thousands of years ago, the goddess Sirius created an animal in her own image to be a companion to the hunters that lived on earth."

"Sirius?" Aden screwed his eyes up in concentration. "Sirius's wolves. My grandparents told me some of the legends, humans call Sirius the Dog Star."

Blaze chuckled and drew comforting circles on Aden's back with his hand. "Humans have adopted the legend and turned it into a domestic animal. The original companion was the ancestor of the wolf, now extinct.

"Human hunters mistreated the animal, it was never taken for the gift it was intended for. It was eventually made feral and Sirius was heartbroken, but after time she relented and tried again to bring humans and the gods together once more. Werewolf shifters were created as a bridge between the two species, half human and half wolf."

Aden studied Blaze while he talked. It was a nice story, but Blaze...it was almost as if Blaze believed every word.

Aden grinned, knowing Blaze had heard his thoughts when the man lifted a sculptured eyebrow. "Technically, I didn't say I didn't believe it, just that you looked like you did."

Blaze smiled and nodded his head in acknowledgement of Aden's point. "The goddess once again had her faith destroyed in humanity. Both species fought for dominance and humans, threatened by the power of the shifters, banded together to destroy them. The existence of werewolves was once again hidden and mostly became the stuff of fairytales and legends. The humans that did know decided to ignore us all together. The story goes that Sirius fell out of favor with the rest of the gods because of her insistence on trying to make a better mankind. They banished her."

"Banish? How can a god be banished?" Aden asked.

"She was banished to the night sky. Her everlasting punishment was to shine every day to see how her experiments had failed."

Aden's heart shrank a little. "That's so sad."

Blaze smiled and kissed Aden's cheek. Aden held his breath; that had been so close to his lips.

"She was granted one last wish before her banishment became permanent. She said that one day when mankind was ready, three werewolves would be created to change the way that man viewed his bigoted existence."

Aden understood by the inflection in Blaze's voice what he meant by the word bigoted.

"Yes, anyone who is not what society expects is therefore shunned. In many countries, homosexuality is still punishable by death, and a lot of wolf packs are as equally narrow-minded, as you know." Blaze added. "It is mankind's last chance to prove itself worthy of the lives the gods have given us."

"Last chance?" Aden didn't like the sound of that.

Blaze sighed. "Legends go that if mankind turns its back on this final effort, humans will be wiped from the face of the earth."

Aden opened his eyes wide. "That's what you are doing?" He gulped. Saving mankind? Aden felt like he'd stepped into an alternate universe.

"It was Sirius's last request, before she was sentenced, that one day werewolves would form an impenetrable bond to work together for the betterment of the human race. Three werewolves—an Alpha triad—had to find something unknown in the whole of the human world before. Until they found it, the circle would never be complete."

"Find what?" Aden could hear his heart beating so loud he wondered why Conner wasn't rushing in thinking he was having a heart attack.

Blaze wrapped both arms around Aden and held him close. "An Alpha triad can only form Orion's Circle when they have the fourth. That fourth has to be special, something unheard of in this world. It is you, Aden, you are Psi. You are our fourth."

Aden gaped, astounded. "But, how do you know all this? I mean, how do you know this is all real?" It wasn't, obviously, but Blaze just watched him with calm eyes. "This Orion's Circle, I mean, and how do you know I'm..." Aden waved his hand, his distress and panic growing.

Blaze caught his hand and slowly brought it to his lips. Aden calmed as the man's warm breath rode his skin. "As pups, Darric, Conner, and I all played together. We were born into a remote pack at the base of the Himalayas in Nepal. It was a poor pack, and the elders were all greatly honored to be visited by the local *trayoti*, or *liberator*. He was the recognized medium to the gods. We were all summoned, much to our disgust." Blaze smiled. "As soon as the *trayoti* saw us, he started wailing and chanting about the reincarnation of Orion's Circle. Not what an eight year old boy wants to witness really, especially when our unusual coloring—Darric and Connor's hair and my blue eyes—already set us apart."

Or your names...

"We Americanized them shortly after we settled here," Blaze answered promptly, and grinned.

Aden shared in Blaze's amusement, and rocked into Blaze's other hand. He had liked the comforting way Blaze rubbed his fingers on his back, and wanted more. Blaze chuckled, and Aden suddenly saw the attraction in Blaze being able to read his thoughts. He tried hard to imagine eight-year-old versions of the three guys. "Are you all the same age?"

Blaze smirked. "We were born within minutes of one another."

Aden's jaw dropped. "B-but." *You don't look anything like each other.*

"We aren't biological triplets, just raised together. Darric's mother was sick for a long time and mine died giving birth to me." Blaze's smile faltered.

"Anyway, the *trayoti* insisted that we be released from the pack to come with him for schooling." Aden felt the wave of disgust from Blaze, and nuzzled his neck in support. He didn't want Blaze to feel any such emotion. He wanted to take it from him. There had been so many times he was forced to take negative emotion, but this he would suffer willingly.

"It doesn't work quite like that with me, little one, but I appreciate the offer." Aden wanted to demand why. Then an awful thought struck him. What if he wasn't worthy of Blaze's emotions? Blaze said Aden wasn't the omega he'd always thought he was.

Aden toed the edge of the chair in frustration. He'd resented being an omega every second of the past three years. Now he was ready to weep because he wasn't a good enough one.

Blaze bent his head so it was in line with Aden's. "I haven't explained properly. It's not that you aren't an omega, it's that you aren't just that. Psi has more powerful abilities than an omega. You become Psi when you mate with us, Aden. My heart hurts that we didn't find you sooner. Will you ever forgive us?"

Aden lifted his head a little in surprise at the words, lined it up more so his lips were resting nearer that full, wide mouth. He inhaled slightly, and caught a scent of something else, something even more amazing than Blaze's usually clean, fresh smell. They were so close, every cell in Aden's body screamed for Blaze's touch. It was as if the world held its breath.

Blaze rested his forehead against Aden's. "You test my reserve." He took a breath and leaned back. "I need to finish my story." Aden sighed, and nodded acquiescence.

"We were 'taught' by the *trayoti* for five years. Our schooling ended when we were thirteen." Aden was surprised, that sounded young to finish school, especially if they were important. "The *trayoti* was unable to finish our teaching."

Aden stared at Blaze. There was a wealth of meaning behind those words. "Why?"

"Because he was dead." Blaze turned and looked unseeing out of the window.

Aden started at the abrupt words. "I'm sorry."

Blaze sighed, and lowered his head slightly against Aden's chest as if seeking comfort. "He was dead because I ripped out his throat." Aden gulped at that, and Blaze zeroed in on the noise. "Aden, I would never—"

Aden melted. "I know." He did know. This huge man should frighten the crap out of him. He could crush him with one hand, but somehow Aden knew he wouldn't. "Finish your story." Aden urged.

"The *trayoti* deserved to die. He knew Darric was *kamuka*." He pulled Aden even closer to cuddle. It was as if Blaze needed the touch also, and he dropped a kiss on Aden's head. "The nearest translation in English of the Nepalese word *kamuka* is sensuous. That is Darric's gift, although in his blacker moments he has seen it as a curse. Any desire he has is magnified a thousand times, and at thirteen it was uncontrollable."

"You mean if he desires"—Aden thought around wildly—"an apple, he absolutely has to have it or someone has to get it for him?"

Blaze threw his head back and laughed out loud. Aden reveled in the sound. "No, beautiful, I mean any *sensuous* feeling, such as the desire to touch, is magnified."

Aden remembered the incredible sexual attraction he felt as soon as Darric had spoken. "You mean he has that effect on everybody?" Aden wrinkled his nose up; he didn't like that thought, didn't like it at all. Blaze smiled. "I know you felt it, couldn't concentrate, that is why I sent them out. It is worse at the moment because the bond between us has started to form, but we have not completed it. We can hear your thoughts unless I prevent them, but you can only hear what we directly say to you, not everything we are thinking. Darric is merely an attractive person to others, engaging, persuasive, not sexually so except unfortunately to deviants wanting their pleasure from little boys."

Aden shook in disgust as the meaning of Blaze's words penetrated. So that was why the *trayoti* was dead. He had tried—"He did only *try*, didn't he?" Aden was nearly crying inside with the thought of what Darric, his Darric, would have gone through.

No. No, I was not fast enough. Blaze said and closed his eyes; Aden watched a forced swallow travel the length of his smooth skin. "He had sent Conner and me to collect firewood deliberately. We had kept our connection with each other a secret, thankfully, and it was only when we heard Darric scream through our link that we knew. His gifts will make him the most powerful negotiator on the planet when the time comes. But sometimes, I think he suffers more than Conner, his desire to touch has overwhelmed him. But now, he has you."

Aden shook his head in distress. He had an incredible urge to have Darric here with them.

"That is your gift, Aden. You offer comfort, without even being aware of it. Have you noticed how Conner calms immediately when you touch him?" Aden nodded. It seemed automatic to him. "That was why the pack kept you for themselves. Properly utilized, an omega is the glue that holds a pack together, and has the most calming influence on its Alpha. In times past, an Alpha would never be allowed to take control without an omega present."

"You said I was more than an omega," Aden said, confused, "but I certainly never seemed to calm Richard down. I seemed to make him worse."

"Psi has all the abilities of an omega, only more so, not less. An omega can only work with one individual. Psi, properly trained, can take the emotions of an entire pack."

"A whole pack?" Aden squeaked, his voice cracking. He shivered in horror. Richard's emotions had hurt so much on their own, but the whole pack?

"It is his evil that hurt you. It's not supposed to hurt at all, but it is incredibly exhausting to the omega, and much more so to a Psi." Blaze frowned. "Something else that is wrong in your old pack I intend to rectify." Aden bent his head back down and inhaled a little. Blaze nuzzled his neck.

"Darric healed me, didn't he?" He flexed his fingers in memory.

Blaze nodded. "Yes, he has that talent, but it can only be used for his mates. He is unable to heal anyone else. Selfishly, I am quite glad because he has to concentrate on other things. Besides which, shifters are rarely in need of it."

"You said that before, but our pack hasn't been able to heal itself by shifting in a long time."

Blaze chewed his lip thoughtfully. "Aden, were your grandparents able to shift and heal? Can you remember?"

Aden shook his head. "No, except I know it was mentioned a few times. My friend Jay—his mother, Ann, used herbs to mix things to help with healing. A lot of families went to her because there was no one else."

Blaze blew a frustrated breath out. "There is something really wrong with your old pack that has caused the healing ability to be lost. I have a meeting with Jefferson pack tomorrow, and we will get some answers." Aden thought about his old pack, and how they had treated him.

"Conner seemed relieved that Alpha Richard didn't know I was Psi. Why? Why did my old pack hate me so much?"

"Richard clearly had some clever advisors," Blaze replied. "I'm not sure, but the pack doctor certainly understands an omega's power. Because Richard was evil, he fed all his hatred and rage into you. You were his focus. If it weren't for you, the entire pack would have been destroyed by the madman. The doctor certainly understands Richard got his kicks from being cruel, and your presence allowed Richard to function effectively. I do not know why the doctor was so invested in Richard remaining Alpha though, and I have yet to see if Craig will be the same as his father or will take a different route."

"But why were they going to kill me if they needed me? I would have been dead if you hadn't been there."

"No, little one. It was an elaborate ruse to be cruel. They would never have killed you. Think, Aden. How powerful was your old pack?"

Aden thought. He did hear things while he was in the cage. "They seemed to be very influential. Alpha Richard was mostly well thought of as we were growing up. We had been told it was only because our Alpha was so strong, he prevented us being slaughtered by Jefferson and our lands from being confiscated."

"He wasn't influential," Blaze said dryly. "He was merely a bully. I think it would have been mostly talk. He was insignificant enough not to have come to the attention of the Jefferson pack, or us until we met you. His power came from you, even though he didn't know it then. But someone knew your worth to the pack and if you were taken away, Richard would have been unable to function. I intend to find out who that was." Aden yawned suddenly, and Blaze smiled. "You should rest. This is a lot to take in."

Aden nodded and stretched his back a little. "I have a few more questions."

Blaze smiled. *Ask away.*

"Mates? You all call me that. I mean—" Aden flushed hotly at the ramifications of being with three men.

"It will not be rushed, little one. Yes, we will enjoy each other, but I promise nothing will happen without your consent and approval."

Aden wasn't worried about that, *at all.* His body had been very much approving all three of them for hours. "You also mentioned we have to bond." Aden felt his face flame as he was sure he knew what Blaze had meant, but...

"The bonding ceremony will happen in nine days."

"Why nine days?" That seemed a very odd number.

"It is exactly nine days until the equinox. There will be a full eclipse, and that hasn't happened for over ninety years." Blaze shook his head in frustration. "I can't believe you're not aware of this, or worse that you can't feel it."

Aden looked down, ashamed. He couldn't even get an apology past the lump in his throat. He was useless. Even though he was a were, he didn't even know when the moon phases were.

Blaze's large hands suddenly tightened and he heard a groan. "Aden, I am so sorry. Of course you wouldn't know. You were held captive."

Startled at an apology, Aden blurted out, "Wait. What did you mean by 'feel it'?"

Blaze settled and pulled Aden nearer. "It angers me that whatever is wrong with your pack seems to include interference with a wolf shifter's basic...psyche, almost." Blaze bent and nuzzled Aden in the crook of his neck. "But it isn't your fault," he added, almost fiercely. "All wolves should be able to feel when the full moon is coming. We can shift, as you know, at any time, but at the full moon the desire is impossible to ignore. For the younger ones—"

"It's like you want to crawl out of your own skin." Aden smiled, suddenly full of understanding. He'd never thought the feeling was due to anything except fear. When his parents and friends went out for the pack runs, his parents had always used the excuse of looking after the little ones to explain his absence. But even though Aden was unable to shift, he had felt the moon's pull.

Blaze nodded. "You do know. I am sorry you had to suffer, but no longer."

"You can't make me shift, Blaze."

Blaze smiled. "I know. Now, you had more questions?"

Aden struggled to voice this one. "You have told me how I can help Darric and I think I know how to help Conner, but what about you?" Aden mumbled the last two words, and his heart seemed to slam in his chest. He would never be worthy of Blaze, never. He couldn't even take his emotion. He—

"You are my center. Never doubt how powerful you are, how much you help. Our Alpha triad can function properly now that you are here. Because I don't need to worry about Darric or Conner, I can focus on what needs to be done."

And Conner?

"Conner is an empath. He can feel emotion a thousand times amplified. He loves more, but he angers quickly and suffers more. You gave him comfort and took that anger almost instantly without even realizing it. Conner will function perfectly, because you..." Blaze smirked. "Will act as his release valve." Blaze kissed Aden's eyelids closed, even though he desperately was trying to keep them open.

Aden was so warm and comfortable. *Stay?*

Blaze stood easily as if Aden's weight was nothing. "I have work to do, but there are two people on their way who are as much in need of your touch as you are theirs."

Aden heard the door open and smiled. The scent of lemons washed over him, as Conner and Darric both walked in and headed for him. Conner's strong arms plucked him from Blaze's, and his head nuzzled Aden's chest.

"He needs to sleep, rest." Aden barely registered Blaze's warning, and as Darric's hands stroked his back, he understood why. He turned his head and pushed open his heavy eyelids to gaze into smiling gray eyes. Darric stripped him of his shirt, and Conner laid him on his side on the bed and pulled his front into his powerful chest, keeping his arms wrapped firmly around him. Aden felt another warm body slide behind him and loop an arm over Conner's, cocooning him between them.

Aden sighed happily, and Darric's lips gently caressed his back. The last thing he was aware of was Darric's chuckle as peace and sleep washed over him.

Chapter Five

Aden heard the grumble from his stomach before he caught the scent of something quite delicious, and it wasn't a man. He heard a snicker from behind him and smiled.

Darric?

"Yes, gorgeous?" Two arms pulled him flush against the warm body that was spooning him, and Aden nearly groaned as he felt Darric's rock hard cock grind his now naked ass.

"There's food waiting for you."

Aden didn't care. He stretched his legs out languorously—it suddenly seemed so...sinful to feel this good. Darric pulled him closer to his chest, his long fingers trailing over his chest. Aden inhaled, Darric's fresh scent warring with what was coming from the large coffee pot on the trolley next to the bed. Aden's stomach growled, and Darric laughed some more.

"I'm losing my touch," he said, squeezing Aden's hip teasingly, then frowned as Aden winced. Darric raised himself up and solemnly turned Aden on his back, pushing Aden's shorts down past his hip.

Aden flushed; he knew what Darric was seeing. Horrible bones sticking out over scarred, tight skin. Aden screwed his eyes shut in disgust. He knew he was ugly.

Aden felt the feather-like touch of a finger to his chin, and he opened his eyes to Darric's calm gaze.

"What happened?" Darric asked.

Aden closed his eyes, couldn't look at Darric while he struggled to find the words. "It wasn't long after they took me. The cage was kept in a corner of the hallway, where I could see the dining room. They used to think it was sport to make me watch them eat when I wasn't allowed to. The hallway was fairly cold, but the dining room was warm. The Alpha used to like a large fire lit in there. He-he asked me if I was warm enough, apologized for keeping me in the cold. It wasn't long after I'd been taken, so I didn't know any better. They'd been drinking, and decided it'd be nice if they could warm me up some. He only had one poker, but they managed to find a couple of tire irons." Aden's voice broke on the last word. He'd screamed. Screamed because he hadn't known any better. Screamed until they'd used the tire iron on his face to shut him up. "My left hip is worse because Gregory told him if he damaged me too bad on both I wouldn't be able to run." Aden's voice was a whisper now. Darric murmured unintelligibly as he gathered him up.

Aden swallowed. Darric was disgusted—he shouldn't have told him. He opened his eyes to apologize but his words stuck in his throat.

Darric was crying. Silent rivulets ran down his skin, and Aden shook, hated that he had been the cause of them, hated the tears for scarring that beautiful face. He tried to wipe them away with his thumb. "Hush. I'm—"

"Don't you dare apologize." Darric took a shuddering breath. "You have nothing to be sorry for."

Darric brushed Aden's face with his fingers and they came away wet, Aden's mouth open in astonishment; he hadn't even realized he was crying. He hadn't cried in a really long time.

Darric cupped his face, gently, but so fiercely. "Never again, Aden." Darric leaned in, their foreheads touching. "Never again."

Aden gulped, smiled at the vehement words, basked in the glow that someone cared, that someone made him feel safe, gloried in the strong arms that wrapped him up, and the soft kisses that bathed his skin. They clung onto each other for a little while, then Darric sat up and reached for the tray.

"Hot chocolate and muffins," Darric said, smiling.

That was an odd thing for lunch, but Aden wasn't complaining. He sat up eagerly. He loved hot chocolate, and he hadn't had it at all in a very long time.

He felt the kiss on the back of his neck as Darric sat up. "You slept straight through, gorgeous. We woke you twice for the bathroom and for water, but I'm not sure if you were even aware of it. You've slept around twenty hours."

"Wow, I was tired huh?" Aden could feel a blush starting in his cheeks, but it wasn't entirely due to him being lazy. Darric's fingers were lightly tracing a path from Aden's neck to his wrist as he seemed incapable of not having some sort of skin contact at all times. Darric hummed and lazily nipped at his shoulder. The slight burn from Darric's teeth zinged down to his cock. Aden gasped at how suddenly hard he was.

The door opened and Conner and Blaze walked in. For a big guy, Conner was surprisingly light on his feet, because he fairly bounced as he walked in the room. Aden could feel the happiness rolling off him in waves, and wondered what had happened.

You woke up, little one, that was what happened.

Blaze's words hit him in the chest. Aden shook his head mutely. How? How did he get this lucky? And when was one of them going to wake up and realize they were fooling themselves? He was...

In two strides Conner was on the bed, nearly pulling him out of Darric's arms. "What's the matter?"

Aden hung his head; he knew the distress and emotion from them both was nearly bouncing off the walls, of course Conner would feel it.

Blaze growled softly, and Darric shook his head once in Conner's direction. Good, because he was never having that conversation ever again, he was done. Conner contented himself with peppering small kisses on Aden everywhere he could reach. Aden caught Conner's lips with his own, burning with a need he couldn't begin to articulate, desperate to touch what he'd never been able to have. If his eyes hadn't been tightly closed in passion, he would have wept with the sheer perfection of that first kiss.

Darric hummed behind him, and that small noise sent a shiver straight to his groin. Aden wrenched his mouth from Conner, wanting to warn him he was so close, but Darric's hand came immediately around and clasped him fairly tight. Aden groaned, the first feel of someone else's hand on his cock other than his own was so goddam perfect, his own hand desperately pressed over Darric's, ignoring the pain and trying to stave off the inevitable for a few more seconds.

Aden was drowning in sensations. Someone gently removed his hand from his cock.

Let me. He barely registered Blaze kneel on the bottom of the bed.

Darric pulled Aden onto his back, and trailed hot, sloppy kisses from his neck to his abs. Conner? Conner found—*Oh, God.* Aden arched as Conner latched onto one of his nipples, and the burst of pleasure was so strong his mouth couldn't contain the cry. Darric immediately lifted his head up and took Aden's lips. Darric's mouth was so soft, the velvet lips teased and tasted, while delicious swipes of his tongue ramped up the desire in Aden's body until he was writhing under the onslaught.

Two mouths on his nipples and his lips took him higher, floating. He no longer had a body, this swirl of sensation and bliss had no corporeal home.

Aden's mind struggled to catch up when the most perfect, stunning, spectacular sensation covered his cock. The vibration when Blaze moaned resonated deep in Aden's body, and he was unable to comprehend the complete and utter perfection in the three seconds before his cock just about exploded into the hot and eager mouth that compelled it to do just that.

The fireworks in Aden's mind echoed the ones behind his eyes until everything was black as he floated, blissed out, convinced he had died a little and heaven had opened for him.

The deep chuckle brought him back, sufficient for him to be aware of being wrapped up protectively and carried once more, the clean scent never leaving him in any doubt that Blaze was carrying him.

"Look." Blaze sat back on the same low chair and Aden cuddled into him shamelessly. He opened one reluctant eye and followed Blaze's stare towards the bed. Aden's mouth fell as he watched the exquisite sight of the two lovers before him.

Conner and Darric were moving to a dance all their own, and it was stunning. Darric's smooth silver head was pinned under Conner's blond one. Darric was moaning, and Conner's soft, needy sounds echoed around the room. Aden's heart bounced in his chest, and his body melted at the incredible sight. He moved restlessly, quickly turned on again, torn between wanting to join them and staying away so as not to interrupt the most beautiful thing he had ever seen.

Blaze groaned underneath Aden once more, and Aden became aware of the man's rock hard cock pushing up between his thighs. Wrenching his eyes from the other two lovers, he eased himself sideways so he could reach Blaze with his hand.

"Oh, Aden," Blaze sighed his name as Aden's smaller fist enclosed his rock hard shaft. Aden turned, hungry for Blaze's mouth, and his tongue slid deep inside, exploring and tasting. Blaze pushed back with his tongue and Aden arched into incredible heat. Blaze wrenched his mouth away and feasted on Aden's neck as Aden leaned back decadently. Aden whimpered as Blaze's tongue danced on his neck, teeth scraping and lips dusting wonder— wonder and ownership. Blaze caught hold of Aden's cock, his rough thumb drawing circles and teasing it to hardness. Aden moaned and shifted on Blaze's lap, trying to get closer. Blaze let go and twisted Aden around so he sat facing him, both legs wrapped around Blaze's waist. Aden wrapped his arms around Blaze's body and fastened his lips back on Blaze's. Aden's head was spinning, and he humped, trying to get closer to Blaze, desperately seeking friction.

"That's mine," Blaze growled as his lips broke off Aden's swollen ones and he reached down, fastening his hand around Aden's leaking cock. Blaze pumped his fist, and Aden gasped as Blaze's other hand came around the back of his neck and pulled him closer. Suddenly, Blaze clamped his teeth into Aden's neck and Aden came again, molten heat pumping from his balls, erupting from his cock. Blaze lifted his cum covered hand to Aden's mouth and without hesitation, Aden's lips closed around his little finger and sucked him clean. Just as Aden was spinning with the taste, Blaze bent his head and sucked one of Aden's fingers.

With a groan Blaze lifted him and walked to the edge of the bed. Blaze lay down next to Darric and Conner while Aden straddled him. The bed was so wide that unless they wished otherwise, both couples had their own space.

Aden leaned forward and rocked into Blaze, reaching back with his fist and wrapping it around Blaze's length, his own cock aching from the stimulation even though he was helpless not to push it forward for friction. Aden moaned as his hands slid in the first trace of the pre-cum on that silky head. He leaned his head back and closed his eyes as another warm pair of lips kissed his back, the slippery feel of Blaze's cock so amazingly good he moaned loud until another mouth caught his.

I love all your noises, beautiful.

Darric. Aden was slammed with desire. In some deep recess of his mind still capable of reason, he knew he was channeling both Conner and Darric, their sensual dance so enmeshed he lost count of whose hands, whose lips, whose bodies were touching and being touched, until all he knew was lust, so perfect and powerful he wanted to be lost in it forever.

Someone's lips blew hot breath against Aden's nipple, and he lifted at the first taste of a sinful tongue. *Mmm...Aden would be stunning with piercings.* Aden molded himself to Darric as the idea took on legs and walked deliciously up his spine.

Pressure built in him and incredibly his balls hardened. He was incredulous knowing he was thundering towards what he knew would be a breathtaking orgasm he didn't think his body would be capable of so soon after the other two.

Seconds before he was about to come, Blaze flipped him on his side to face him. He couldn't see but he knew Darric lay behind Blaze, and as Blaze pushed back into Darric with a roar, he almost felt the moment of penetration, as Darric's perfect shout echoed around the room and his mind. At the same time Blaze's hand encased Aden's pulsing cock, and Conner's slick shaft pushed behind him, too low to penetrate, but high enough for friction.

Aden exploded with pleasure, and Blaze's lips met his.

Aden opened his eyes, blinking in a tangle of arms and legs, and cold, sticky cum. His lungs heaved to inhale oxygen, and he became aware of Blaze's hands painting cum on his chest, while Conner, from the feel, was doing the same to his back.

"You are being marked." Blaze's words were solemn, but his eyes were kind.

"It is our promise to you that you belong to us, and we to you." Darric rose and reached over, wiping some of the cum from Aden's chest and trailing a finger around his lips. Conner's gaze followed Darric's movement, until Darric lifted his head and a slow smile seemed to bathe Conner's face. Aden reveled in the intensity of their connection, and then as one they both turned and smiled at him.

Blaze turned his head and looked at Darric, his eyes gleaming in satisfaction. Aden was reminded of them a few minutes ago and struggled with the surprise of what he thought had happened. Conner chuckled behind him. "We are all Alphas, gorgeous. It is as much an honor to allow as to *do*." Darric smiled wickedly.

"But, Blaze is..." Aden's words trailed off in embarrassment. He was very much afraid he had just insulted Darric and Conner.

Blaze laughed, and cupped Aden's face to bring it nearer for a brief kiss. "We are a circle. There is no end and no beginning. We are only powerful when we are together, stronger when we are together. I may have greater strength, but only because I can take it from the power we generate as a whole."

Aden still struggled with his thoughts though. Blaze was huge, but then so was Darric. Conner was slimmer, but still powerfully built. Conner laughed out loud. "Aden, I don't mean physical strength, although Blaze is the only one of us that could take that from both of us if he needed to supplement his own. I mean mental strength, strength of mind. That is why he will lead. He hasn't the same distractions as the rest of us to pull his focus away."

Aden suddenly understood. Darric's sensuality dialed down to attractiveness would make him more appealing to strangers, essential in dealing with the mistrust of the humans they had to negotiate with. Conner's empathic abilities would tell Blaze of the humans' honesty and Aden... What had Blaze called him?

He grinned. *A release valve.* Three voices laughed in his head.

Aden sat up ruefully, and looked at the cold sticky mess. "So, you got a shower we can all fit in?"

The sharp stab of lust and echoing growls gave him his answer.

Chapter Six

Aden was stuffed. He placed his hands ruefully over what he'd just managed to cram into his belly, and idly wondered how long the new clothes Blaze kept bringing him would still fit. In the last two days he'd been cossetted, fussed over, and plied with all manner of wonderful things to eat. He'd met Lilly, the cook. She was mated to the smaller man, Ben, who seemed to help Blaze with all the business things he had to do.

"You're all going to make me fat," he complained.

Darric hummed. "A little pot belly would make you so cute though."

Aden raised horrified eyes and Conner chuckled. Darric reached over and snagged a banana. He broke it in half and offered a piece to Aden. Aden shuddered—he hated bananas. Darric grinned.

The door opened and Ben walked into the imposing dining room. He had some business papers he needed Blaze to sign. Aden looked around the large opulent space, wondering what they did for work. He hadn't spent much time in the last two days doing much except eating and sleeping, but now that he felt better, curiosity was overtaking him.

He smiled and thanked the two women who came in to clear the food away. The first time that had happened, he had risen to help, only to be beaten back by the horrified exclamations of both women. It was incredible really, after being treated like scum for so long, he was nearly revered as royalty here. He grinned. He'd better not let that thought go to his head.

Blaze shot an apologetic look at Aden and followed the man out of the room. Conner leaned back with his coffee and glanced at Darric. Darric nodded as if answering an unspoken question.

"What do you all do here?" He'd watched the construction going on outside the window, and suddenly wondered how they were paying for it. Aden winced. What a question, he really had to remember they could hear his thoughts.

Conner looped Aden's arms around him, lifted, and settled on the corner chair, cuddling Aden close.

Darric smiled. "I will let you explain that one, I need to help Blaze." He looked at Aden. "Actually, I think a tour would be better," and he nodded, satisfied.

Aden watched Darric leave the room and settled into Conner. He couldn't help it, but it seemed easier to talk just to Conner sometimes.

"That is kind of a cheat really, although I'm not complaining."

"A cheat?" Aden murmured, contentment stealing over him. God, he was happy, why on earth had he worried about asking them anything?

He heard the low rumble in his mind, and rather than soothe, it suddenly made him more alert. He instantly knew what Conner was doing.

Well done for being so perceptive.

"It's you, isn't it? You're making me feel so...*unworried?*"

Conner laughed. "I'm an empath. I channel emotions, and that's why I anger easily. It feeds into me."

Aden tilted his head. "And that's why I can soothe you easier? The emotions channel both ways?"

Conner nodded. "The only reason you cannot hear all our thoughts immediately is because we have not completed the bonding. We can merely 'talk' to you at present."

"I—" Aden blushed crimson. He was just about to protest and say he felt very bonded with all of them considering the sticky mess they had washed off each other more than once in the shower in the last two days, when he suddenly remembered some of the bonding ceremonies from his old pack, and winced. Bonding at Black Lakes had always just been a lesson in humiliation, the couple fucking as humans in front of the whole pack, and there was no way...

Conner put his head back and roared with laughter.

Aden blushed. *I have two questions.* He looked at Conner, hopefully. He definitely couldn't ask one of them out loud.

"So, start with your easiest," Connor said. Aden sighed in exasperation as he saw Conner doing his best to paint a serious face on.

"What do you actually do here?" *If you're not running a pack.*

"Orion's Circle will be the ruling center for all werewolves. Whist we expect individual Alphas to govern their own packs, we want to regulate a lot of things. Punishment, opportunities for development."

"Like the military thing?" Aden interrupted.

Conner nodded. "Yes, but we have a lot of young people desperate to go into other human fields—medicine, government, technology. That's what we will do. The military is just a first step to show our willingness to help safeguard the world we want to share. For years, shifters have pretended the outside world and its troubles don't exist."

Conner smiled. *And the second question?*

"What does the, um...bonding actually entail?" Aden nearly closed his eyes against the flush he could feel starting in his neck.

He felt a gentle kiss on his cheek. "I'm sorry, Aden. I shouldn't have laughed. The part of the bonding you are speaking of *will* take place, but in private only. Sirius told us when we found our Psi, she would bond us together. We're kind of guessing on some sort of ceremony, but we haven't done this before either."

"I have a third question." Aden looked beseechingly at Conner, hoping he wasn't going to have to say it out loud, but what about him and Conner, or him and Darric?

Conner nuzzled his cheek. "Technically," Conner paused and laughed at his choice of word. "Technically you only have to bond with Blaze for Orion's Circle to be formed, but it's something, um, we can think about later." Aden stared into Conner's warm brown eyes and felt his cock stirring once again. It was definitely something he wanted to think about later. Aden gulped. Was Conner really going to make him ask the question?

Conner's face gentled. "I'm sorry, I shouldn't tease. But yes, you are right, you also have to complete the bonding with Blaze."

Aden's mind whirled, and forgetting his shyness he opened his mouth to ask more questions.

A knock on the door interrupted them, and Ben entered. Aden scrambled to his feet as Conner stood. Aden felt Conner tense. "What is it, Ben?"

"Sir, Alpha Blaze needs you both."

Ben sounded serious and Aden hurried to keep up to Conner's long strides as he left the room. Aden glanced around quickly as they walked. He'd not taken much notice before when Blaze had carried him from the room, but now he peered out of the windows as they passed, and could see a lot of dense woodland surrounding where they were. He wondered if they were still in the area of Lost Creek he had been chased into. He really had to get some more information, and start asking some questions. He swung his head towards Conner's rapidly retreating back. He felt Conner's worry, but he still didn't have the strength to keep up with Conner's giant strides. They rounded a corridor and Conner started up some wide, bare wooden steps two at a time.

Conner. Aden huffed in frustration.

Conner turned suddenly, as if Aden's thoughts finally penetrated his brain. He immediately looked horrified, and strode back to Aden. "I am so sorry."

He picked Aden up in his arms. *Just until we get to the top of the stairs.*

Aden acquiesced reluctantly at Conner's reassurance. Whatever was wrong, he couldn't help if he arrived thirty minutes after everybody else. He was going to get fit again if it killed him. He felt the rueful apology again from Conner as he put Aden down outside two huge wooden doors.

What is it, Conner? What's wrong?

I don't know. Blaze's thoughts are...worried.

Conner pushed the door open and clasped Aden's hand as he walked in. *This is not to embarrass you, I need to feel you.*

Aden nodded. At that moment he didn't care what it looked like. He needed to feel Conner too.

Humans.

Aden caught the scent of the men at once, he didn't need Conner's confirmation. The room was full of several people, mostly dressed in business suits. They were seated around a large conference table with Blaze at its head, and two gammas stood by the doors at the far end.

He glanced at Blaze's face as he entered and nearly gasped. He'd seen passion, kindness, humor, and desire flit across it many times in the last two days, but he'd never seen such anger. He glanced at the other unperturbed faces in the room, and back to Blaze's hard mask. Aden blinked. They couldn't see Blaze was angry, as that smooth face gave nothing away, but he could feel every thud and dive of Blaze's heart. Two strides and he was by Blaze's side, gratified at feeling the approval from Conner.

He pressed into Blaze's side silently, and focused on the speaker. It was a woman. She seemed to be head of a delegation of some sort.

"We have all the other surrounding packs' agreement of course." The condescending tone of the woman dripped from her thin, bright red lips. Aden watched the pulse point jump erratically in her lined neck, and was reminded of a landed fish, when the scales heaved emptily for water. He glanced at Darric when he heard the soft chuckle in his mind, but he didn't smile, he knew this was serious.

The woman seemed fascinated with her nails, slashed the same unattractive blood red color as her lips. "Of course," she continued, "your pack being the smallest, doesn't warrant the same level of consideration that we are offering

Black Lakes, and Jefferson County. But, we are eager to make this a smooth transaction."

Aden nearly gasped as he caught sight of one of the taller men moving subtly, displaying a holstered gun.

Conner spoke in his head. *There is no immediate danger, Aden. They would have been prevented entrance.*

Aden blew a long, unhurried breath out of his nose. Of course. Conner would be able to sense any immediate threat from the humans.

Blaze pressed slightly into Aden, and Aden was bathed with comfort. He nearly shook his head in exasperation. He wanted to offer strength and support to Blaze, not the other way around.

You do, little one, every damn second.

Aden had no time to think of a reply since Blaze started talking again. "Senator Addison, while I appreciate your apparent need to satisfy yourself we are no threat in your desire to harness werewolf strength for your military ambitions, please make no mistake over one thing. You are not standing before a small pack. In fact, you are not standing before a pack at all. You are looking at the ruling council of werewolves for all of North America, and henceforth you will no longer be welcome into our immediate lands without an invitation and a werewolf escort."

Aden managed to keep his lips firmly closed, despite naturally wanting to drop his bottom jaw in astonishment at Blaze's words. *All werewolves of North America? Ruling Council?* Despite Blaze's explanation earlier, he still hadn't realized their importance. Instantly, as if Blaze had commanded it, the doors at either end of the long room opened and wolves streamed in to stand behind Blaze, Darric, and Conner. Aden could nearly taste the immediate tension ramp up in the room, and more than one human reached for his gun.

"My wolves would take the throats from your men before they finished the thought of going for their guns."

Aden cheered silently when the Senator gulped visibly and shook her head. The humans dropped their hands from their guns.

"You will be escorted from our lands. A boundary has already been indicated, and details have been sent to your office to make our stipulations about unwanted visitors clear."

The Senator drew herself up as if to speak, but Blaze continued.

"An invitation has already been issued to one of the Senate Armed Services Subcommittee to discuss the strategy needed for adapting military procedures to include wolves." Senator Addison clearly didn't have the same control as Aden, as her mouth gaped unattractively at Blaze's words.

Aden felt her eyes rake furiously over Blaze, and even worse, her disdain, as she took in how Aden was firmly plastered into Blaze's side.

Darric and Conner both growled low in warning, but Aden didn't need to have empathic abilities to feel the waves of disgust that radiated from the Senator.

Aden immediately touched Conner and Darric as they stood closer. He almost grinned as he saw the fury in the Senator's gaze over the display of intimacy.

Without so much as a backward glance the woman jerked her head at her men and stormed out of the doors. Within seconds, Aden was completely surrounded by all three of his mates.

Guys, a little oxygen here. Aden grinned as he felt the amusement, knowing his mildly sarcastic tone had dissipated some of the tension from all three of them, but they still kept close. Darric especially seemed to need Aden to be close, and Aden calmly leaned back into his chest, bleeding the tension out of Darric until he heard the soft sigh.

Thank you.

Aden calmly took Darric's very willing arms and wrapped them around his abdomen in answer.

Darric waited while Blaze thanked and dismissed everyone, then whispered to Aden, "You see, you have far more strength than you give yourself credit for." Aden smiled serenely as he felt Darric's insistent length grow and press harder against his buttocks.

Being a release valve wasn't that bad. All three of his mates laughed out loud.

Darric lifted his face from Aden's neck and looked at Blaze. "Did you have to tell that ridiculous woman about our plans?" Darric sounded almost bored, but Aden had wondered that himself.

Blaze chuckled. "Ignore Darric, Aden. He knows full well she would have been here anyway, she's on the Emerging Capabilities Committee. This is what all this is about, she's hoping to get a jump on the whole thing."

"So why was she here then, if the defense people are meeting anyway?"

"Because she's very insignificant to the large group that will be here tomorrow, and she wants to exert her authority. We are negotiating for the inclusion of werewolves in the military. It's been coming on for some time, not only because individual weres have that sort of ambition which has been previously denied to them, but because werewolves themselves can no longer pretend they exist in a bubble untouched by terrorism and all the evil in this world."

Darric interrupted Blaze. "But we need it on our terms for obvious reasons, mates, humans understanding that full moon runs have to be figured into military operations, shifting into their wolves even."

Aden's head was spinning. He couldn't grasp the enormity of what they were planning. "And all weres approve of this? Jefferson?"

Conner smiled. "Let's show you around, we can answer questions as we go."

They showed Aden around most of the pack area, and they had trailed slowly over most of the large house. Apparently, it had been built over a hundred years ago by a very wealthy family until Blaze, Darric, and Conner had decided to settle here and purchased it, along with the surrounding three hundred acres just south-west of Denver. Aden was amazed as he saw all the building work going on outside the windows as they passed houses and common areas. Finally, they had just gotten to the front of the house, a huge empty space.

"What's this area going to be for?" Aden's mind was already alive with possibilities. The main house seemed to have been neglected in favor of everything else.

Blaze shrugged. "We haven't thought about it."

Darric put in. "But you are, aren't you, Aden?"

Aden nodded. He eagerly explained his ideas for a welcome area for anyone from the pack to just "hang out". There could be somewhere to eat, and somewhere for the kids to play. It's what he'd always wished for in his old pack, but never thought he'd get the chance to see.

Blaze looked pleased. "That would work, especially with the families of the wolves who will be guarding the compound at that particular time." They all stepped outside.

There were a lot of guys working. "Are they all wolves?" Aden looked around him. Some he could scent as shifters, some not. Blaze hadn't smelled "wolf" to him at all.

"Yes, these are all sent from Jefferson. But it is our intention to have our own community here eventually."

"And to answer your question," Blaze interrupted Darric, "the wolves that have the strongest scent are generally the oldest. Some packs smell different, but lack of scent is also an indication of pure lines."

Aden frowned, and Conner added, "Blaze doesn't smell of pack because he is a direct descendant of the first ever wolf shifter." He grinned and nudged Aden. "Your pack was just plain nasty."

Aden looked at Conner, horrified, and tried to inhale unobtrusively. Oh God, he didn't smell like his old pack, did he? Richard had been putrid.

Darric laughed and the other two joined him. "Don't worry, it was your clean smell that attracted Conner to you in the first place. You were the only thing in that clearing that didn't smell like it had died weeks ago."

Conner huffed. "Present company excluded of course." He snagged Aden's hand.

Aden squeezed his back automatically. He loved the constant touching from them. It was as if they both needed him. He glanced over at Blaze who was talking to one of the workmen. Sometimes Blaze seemed very distant. Conner squeezed his hand.

Aden watched as four men heaved, and set out partially built timber frames ready to erect. "Jefferson pack are helping you do all this?" Aden was astounded the Jefferson Alpha wasn't taking this as a direct challenge.

"We have met the Jefferson Alpha and his betas regularly over the last year when we chose to settle here. He is a very wise man and understands how he fits within our plans. While we have a superior strength, he knows we are no threat to him, and we have Jefferson's support and loyalty." Darric smiled. "He was very reasonable to negotiate with. Intelligent men usually are."

"You aren't forming your own pack?"

"No," Blaze put in, walking back to join them. "Any wolves who wish to settle permanently are welcome, but the compound will be secured by a roving deputation from different packs. We cannot show preference to one, and all must demonstrate their loyalty."

"But how?" Aden was still unconvinced. A pack was powerful because of its combined strength, everyone knew that.

"We have met some of the elders before," Darric said.

Aden glanced expectantly at all of them, and he grinned when he heard the chuckles.

Blaze carried on walking. "We will explain later."

Aden nodded happily. He didn't need proof. To be honest, so long as he could always stay here with them, it didn't matter if they were powerful or not. He leaned back into Darric's strength, tired after they had been walking for a while.

Blaze zeroed in on him. "I think a rest is due."

They walked back slowly towards the house. Conner's enthusiasm bubbled over as he pointed out in the distance the newly built landing strip and hangars for their private jets and helicopter.

"Just how rich are you guys?" Aden finally blurted out, and blushed at Blaze's laugh.

Millionaires, smirked Conner, smugly.

Darric shook his head. "Conner gets a feel for certain investments," he explained, his eyes crinkling in amusement.

Aden looked at Conner in astonishment. "Are you saying you can tell something is going to be successful?"

Conner grinned. "I can sense skill, determination, and honesty." His mood dialed back a little. "I can also sense dishonesty and greed, so it gives me an advantage in the stock market."

"It's not just that," added Blaze. "He's actually very perceptive, and seems to have a knack for investments, even without the advantage of knowing who is behind them."

Conner's face fell slightly, and Aden felt the cold in his expression. He knew something was wrong and immediately walked into Conner's arms. Conner bent and nuzzled his neck.

Can I help? Aden didn't want Conner to suffer anything if he could stop it.

Conner brought his head up. "It happened a long time ago. I urged investment in something that turned out to be quite immoral."

"But we made reparations," said Darric. Conner nodded, and Darric added, "There is a school built where there was once an ammunitions factory."

They headed back to the house, and Aden paused as he heard giggling noises from behind a group of bushes.

Conner shot an amused look at Darric, and Blaze silently replaced Conner at Aden's back. Conner and Darric each crept around the bushes from different sides and suddenly dived. Squeals and giggles erupted, and Darric and Conner appeared each holding a wriggling mass of humanity. Aden grinned delightedly. He hadn't seen happy kids in a very long time. *Red*, happy kids. Their fingers and cheeks—even their clothes—looked like they had been drenched in red paint.

"No, no, Darric. Let me go." A furious, squirming little girl with red hair and far more freckles than any one person had a right to, wriggled until Darric deposited her gently in a huff on the grass.

Her companion, a younger looking boy with just as many freckles, clasped his hand over his mouth as his horrified eyes widened. "Ooh, Cassie, you're gonna be in so much trouble. You know Mom said we had to call Darric, Alpha."

The redhead rounded on who Aden assumed was her brother. "Well, you just called Darric, Darric," she pointed out triumphantly, and her brother was lost for words. He shot a nervous look at the silver-haired giant, but Darric just put his head back and roared with laughter.

Conner put a gentle arm around the little boy. "Word of advice, Brantley. Never argue with a female."

Lilly appeared around the corner then carrying a basket of strawberries, and at that point Aden realized where the red stains decorating both kids had come from. "Cassie, Brantley—neither of you are gonna get any strawberry ice cream if you eat them all now."

"Mom." Brantley sidled up to Lilly, and Cassie muttered something about just testing them. Lilly sent a smile in Aden's general direction and bustled her kids toward the kitchen.

Aden was charmed, and swallowed around the lump in his throat. He remembered picking berries as a child, and eating more than went into the basket, but with his dad. His dad always insisted his mom could burn water and always did the cooking for their family.

When they'd still had one.

Aden fought not to remember the Alpha's words when his parents had finally been summoned to see the Alpha, after being denied access to him for months, and he'd been duly beaten in front of them. As he'd felt his ribs go, the Alpha had mockingly told him he had a birthday surprise and he'd vaguely realized it was his birthday—he was eighteen. He must have passed out because when the gammas threw the cold water at him to wake him up, it was his mother's screams he had heard as his father was torn in two in front of them both. Then when his mother met the same fate, he wished for death himself. He hadn't been that lucky.

Darric's strong arms stopped him from hitting the floor and his kisses brushed away the moisture from his face. Conner murmured soothing words, desperate to chase away the horror in his mind. Aden tried to calm himself down. He could feel Darric's soothing touch weave through him and desperation fading into sadness. He took a shuddering breath, and gazed up at the three worried faces of his mates.

"I'm sorry."

All three faces frowned and Aden couldn't help a little smile. He stood straighter. "Before you say it, I know I don't need to apologize exactly." He studied each of them. Gray eyes that were now smiling lazily at him, Darric's firm wide mouth breathing warmth on his neck, and teasing, erotic thoughts dappling his flesh like a cool breeze. The warm, brown eyes of Conner smiling at him, telling him they would always have his back no matter what he did; the strong blue ones of his Alpha that saw everything, and still wanted him.

Chapter Seven

Aden walked into their rooms, followed by Blaze, Darric, and Conner, and flopped into one of the overstuffed chairs that had appeared in the corner. The large space had been completely empty, but yesterday a couch and two chairs had appeared, making the area very cozy. Aden approved.

Blaze immediately picked him up and settled back down in the chair. Aden smiled, half in exasperation. They made him feel like a child.

There is absolutely nothing remotely child-like about my current feelings.

Aden grinned at Blaze and ground his hips teasingly a little into the man's massive thighs. Blaze had kept a certain distance for the last couple of days, and Aden was starting to feel it. Blaze wrapped his arms around Aden and nuzzled his neck.

Conner sat next to Darric on the sofa. Darric pulled the man towards him until Conner lifted his legs completely onto the sofa and lay cushioned against Darric. Darric played with his hair softly.

"We always knew one day it would come to this," Blaze said as Aden settled into his arms, watching Darric. "The *trayoti* was wrong in a lot of things." Darric paused and speared Aden with a gaze. Aden gasped at the pain he saw in those eyes; Conner made a small hurt sound in the back of his throat, and put his hand on the bigger man's leg.

Darric smiled softly down at Conner. "Peace, my friend. It was a long time ago."

He glanced back at Aden. "But all his visions for the future have been correct so far."

"Like what?" Aden was curious. "Orion's Circle?" He felt Blaze nod in confirmation. "What other visions did he have?"

"The Great War was a favorite, as I remember." Conner added drily. Aden sat a little higher. "The Great War? There is a war coming?" Darric glanced at Blaze and subsided. Aden felt Blaze take a breath. "There is a war of sorts coming, but that was not the one the *trayoti* spoke of."

Aden twisted so he could look into Blaze's blue eyes. "So which war did he mean, then?"

He felt another sigh from Blaze. "He meant the first world war in 1914." Aden frowned. "I don't understand. How can you prophesy something that has already happened? I mean..." He grinned. "Anyone could do that."

Blaze fixed Aden with a calm look. "He told us five hundred years before the war had started."

Aden gaped. "Five...five hundred years?" He stared back at Blaze, glanced at the equally solemn faces of Darric and Conner. "But—" *That's impossible.* He gulped. "Just how old are you guys?"

"Six hundred and thirteen," Darric replied.

Conner punched Darric playfully. "You two speak for yourselves. I wasn't born until past midnight, remember? I'm a whole day younger." He grinned at Aden and huffed. "Old men, huh?"

Aden heard Blaze's laugh behind him, and shook his head slightly in complete disbelief. "You're over six hundred years old?" His voice squeaked and he twisted around to glare at Blaze, as if it were his fault.

Conner nodded. "We are."

Aden gulped, trying to bank his hysteria down a little. "But how is that even possible?"

"The *trayoti* told us Sirius's wolves would be blessed with the years necessary to get the job done. We honestly have no idea how long we will live for."

Darric tweaked Conner's ear fondly. "You don't look a day over thirty-five."

Conner put on a mock-horror expression at Darric's words. "That old?"

Aden pulled out of Blaze's grip and stood on shaky legs. He couldn't wrap his head around this at all. He remembered his grandfather, barely. He had been sad when the old wolf had died, but his mom had told him one hundred and seventy-two years was old for a wolf and he had had a good life.

He remembered snatches of their conversation, the way they spoke, especially Blaze. He'd assumed it was from being born in a foreign country, not because Blaze was over six hundred years old.

The scent of lemons wafted over him as he felt warmth at his back. "Does this bother you?"

Aden turned. He could feel the worry from Conner layer over his skin. Aden softened immediately and stepped forward into Conner's arms. How could he explain what he was worried about?

Ah, little one. He heard a small understanding sound from Darric at the same time as Blaze's words in his head.

Blaze sighed. Aden raised his head just in time to catch a worried shake of the head from Darric.

"What is it? What else haven't you told me?"

Blaze smiled. "I know this is hard to take in."

Blaze wasn't answering him. Darric hesitated. "Aden, you will likely live for a long time also. More so than an ordinary wolf life span." He chewed his lip and glanced at Blaze.

"Sirius's legend states that Orion's Circle is needed to bring the balance that mankind desperately needs. Terrorism? Al-Qaeda? Your pack was closed, but even you must be aware of the horrors the world is facing." Blaze paced, frustrated. "We simply don't want to overwhelm you with the responsibility until you have had time to consider this."

"Blaze," Darric growled the warning.

Blaze stopped pacing, and pinned Darric with a glare. "You know how important this is." Darric nodded silently, and Blaze turned back to Aden. "When we bond you will be given sufficient years like us to get the job done. I am trying to give you time. I don't want to pressure you, but the world is in crisis, and we were put here to do a job."

Aden gulped, the enormity of their task weighing heavily on him, and it wasn't that he didn't think they weren't very worthy of the responsibility. "What if I'm not good enough?" he blurted out. "You're all Alphas. You're immortal for God's sake. How am I ever going to live up to that?" Aden pinned Blaze with a glare. "I'm a joke. I always have been. Even you three joke about me." *Release valve.* Even they didn't take him seriously.

A large hand cupped his face and thumbed away the tears that Aden hadn't realized he was making. "Aden." It was Conner. He felt the man hold him tight and press a kiss on the back of his neck. "You were made for us."

"You were," Blaze urged and crouched down in front of Conner.

Darric smiled, and stood behind Blaze. "And we're not immortal, and neither are you. So don't go doing anything silly." Aden shook his head in exasperation as Blaze growled softly in agreement at Darric's words.

Blaze licked his lips and put his hand on Aden's leg. "You have to understand, everything's different now. You're different now. You are blessed by the goddess Sirius, and were made for us. You are Psi, powerful and compassionate. You are important, especially to us." Blaze rubbed the palm of his hands over Aden's pants, traced his finger down the seam of his zipper.

Aden trembled in Conner's arms, but not in fear. He'd seen the desire in Blaze's eyes. Blaze was right. This was what he had been made for. This feeling of belonging. This feeling of passion. The sudden desperate need to lie in another's arms, to have another's hands touch his body, another's fingers smooth his cock, and another's lips cover his. Aden made a small, desperate sound in the back of his throat as he was turned away from Conner's embrace and was pulled flush into Blaze's. The sound was not in protest though, it was from his mind reeling with the conviction that he had never needed anything so much in his life as Blaze's touch. Lust slammed into Aden, robbed him of all breath. Growls echoed around the room as two large hands cupped his ass and wrenched him up and forward. He wrapped his legs around Blaze's waist in desperation to be closer, almost crying with the frustration of being still clothed, clawing at Blaze's shirt.

Hot lips caught his. A wet tongue plundered every recess of his mouth, slowly, measured, as if Blaze had all the time in the world to kiss Aden, and to be kissed back. Aden moaned, echoing the soft sounds from the hot body pressed up to his.

He shivered as his shirt was eased upwards and smooth kisses were pressed along his spine. He wanted to arch into the sensations, but couldn't bear to leave those lips. He felt Blaze move, and another pair of hands guide them towards the bed. His head was swimming with lazy thoughts of being undressed slowly inch by perfect inch. He knew Darric was showing those to him, telling him in images and feelings just what he was going to do. Blaze pulled him in tighter but Darric's fingers turned Aden's head and he captured his lips.

Lover. Mine.

Aden was barely aware of who had spoken, but his body was screaming *yours* as he was laid on the bed. Aden scrambled up as Blaze lay down. Blaze was too calm, too controlled.

I don't want to hurt you.

Aden hesitated and his confidence plummeted along with his desire. Who was he kidding? He wasn't desirable, he was fooling himself.

"Stop. Stop." Darric caught him as he was just about to break away. "Aden, we have been waiting for you for so long. Whatever made you think that we do not ache to be with you every single second of every day?"

"I knew from the second I scented you in the clearing." Conner said.

"We all did. Conner first because he was the nearest to you." Blaze sat up and rubbed a thumb along Aden's jaw. "You have been treated badly for months, and you need to heal."

Aden lifted hopeful eyes to Blaze.

Conner wrapped an arm around him. "Do you have any idea how impossible it has been for us to leave you any second of the last few days?"

"You're still not fully healed," Darric growled low, and Aden felt deep pain and frustration echo around the room.

Blaze stared at Aden. "We have told you how we feel, how we ache to have you with us."

"But only with your consent," Conner added urgently. "It would never be anything else."

Blaze nodded. "That is very important. You do not have to stay with us out of fear of your old pack. You will always be safe with or without the bond, and if you so choose, we can relocate you anywhere you wish. Accepting our bond will change your life. It is not something to be taken lightly."

Darric leaned in. "It would kill me if for one second you thought your survival depended on accepting us. You will never go back to your old pack, no matter what you choose."

Aden looked at the three faces staring at him. He reached for Darric, and the man's gray eyes glowed before he bent his head and breathed a kiss on Aden's palm. A small sound made him turn his head to see the soft brown eyes of Conner shimmer with worry. Aden breathed and drew the emotion in as he reached for Conner's hand, until his eyes shone bright and Aden let it go.

Then he turned to Blaze. This man—possibly the most powerful wolf on the planet—wanted him, needed him. His heart hurt with the thought of not being with these three forever. He made a tiny move forward, almost a plea, but Blaze was faster.

"Undress him."

The low order rippled through Aden's body like a wave. Darric and Conner slowly began to strip him. Blaze's look never faltered and Aden trembled at the desire in those depths. Darric and Conner caressed each inch of his bared skin, their hands gentle, their lips even softer. Aden gasped as his pants were unbuttoned, the lust from Darric nearly buckling his knees.

Blaze stripped in seconds and stretched out on the bed. His cock jutted up proudly, and as Conner and Darric's strong hands lifted Aden, Blaze widened his legs for him to kneel in the space between them.

Blaze's eyes burned, and Aden suddenly knew what to do. He leaned forward and nuzzled hesitantly in the soft as silk hair that bathed Blaze's groin. Blaze gasped at the touch of Aden's tongue, and Aden arched as he felt the man's hands stroke his buttocks. He wasn't going to last, much as he desperately wanted to; even the thought of tasting the bead of moisture that had formed on the tip of the man's powerful cock sent his body into overdrive.

"Then let us take the edge off first," Conner murmured. He lifted him and in seconds Aden was flat on his back. Blaze lay at his side and when he dipped his head and fastened his lips over one of Aden's nipples, Aden thought he would stop breathing. Darric chuckled softly and knelt on the bed below him. Conner pulled both Aden's legs up, knees bent, feet flat on the bed. He lay sideways to Aden, and before Aden could wrap his mind around what he was about to do, Conner put his arm under both of Aden's thighs to hold them there, and bent his head to capture Aden's cock from the side.

"Conner. I—" Aden couldn't speak; he nearly couldn't breathe. All intelligent thought sped out of his brain until at the last second when he thought he was in heaven, absolute perfection happened as another tongue touched his hole. Heat shimmered, and stars burst behind his eyes as he arched into hands and mouths, unable to halt or stave off the powerful orgasm that barreled into him.

Aden lay panting, hyper aware of every cell in his body. Blaze nuzzled his neck and twirled a finger around his sensitive nipple. "You're not going anywhere. We only just started."

He felt lips kiss his still hard cock. "That was just so you could last a little longer." Conner said. The man's lips moved in a smile against his skin.

"We may need you for hours. We—" Darric's words cut off as Conner reached his hand around the back of Darric's head and pulled him forward for a kiss.

You taste amazing. Aden's lips parted as he heard Blaze's words. *You do.* Blaze pulled his mouth down to meet his, as his hand slid down to where Blaze could wrap both their lengths in his large hand. It hurt, briefly, as his cock struggled after being used to nothing except his own hand, and lately, not even that.

He felt the low possessive growl from Blaze, and nearly laughed that he could please him with something so simple as being his first. The pain in his cock suddenly molded into something else, and desire walked his spine and danced on his abdomen. He could hear the needy moans from Darric and Conner getting more urgent with each other. Low murmurs from them both filled the room and hands caught his skin. He latched onto Blaze's warm mouth, and reveled in his touch. Blaze broke free as another warm body closed in nearer to him. It was Conner, and Aden sighed into his touch.

Blaze shuffled nearer his feet and nodded to Conner. Conner tightened the arm raising Aden's legs. He tensed—he couldn't help it. Blaze was huge.

I promised not to hurt you. Blaze said.

But how could you not?

"Because we will make you so delirious with need it will be all you can concentrate on." Darric's low voice echoed around the room and Aden felt like he was sinking a foot further into the bed. He barely heard anything else as Darric's gray eyes pinned him in place and more of his soft words washed over him.

His hole clenched reflexively as Blaze's traced lazy circles with his finger around Aden's rim. He wrenched worried eyes away from Darric.

"Look at me." Darric palmed his cheek and gently drew him back. "Don't worry. Just concentrate on the feel of Conner's mouth and listen to me."

Aden blinked slowly and settled further into those mesmerizing gray eyes. They seemed to burn right through him. He relaxed as delicious kisses fluttered across his abdomen and thighs. All the while gentle fingers continued their lazy circles as inch by inch Aden relaxed against them, Conner's mouth, and Darric's words.

"I can feel you in here." Darric lifted Aden's hand and pressed it to his chest. "You belong. We belong." Aden gasped and his head reared back in wonder as Conner's firm lips surrounded his hard, leaking cock. He strained unbelievably at the tip of Blaze's finger as it probed his ass, teasing, with a delicious scraping sensation from Blaze's nail.

"You have such beautiful nipples." Darric murmured, and bent his head to pull at one with his teeth. Aden was lost, his mind completely blown with the waves of sensuality that were breaking over him. All thought and worry left him. It was if he was on a different plane of existence where the only touch possible was one of pleasure, and the only words he heard were the hot whispers from Darric. He heard the click of the lube Blaze was going to use, simply overwhelmed with the urgent need for...something. He moaned long and low as he shifted restlessly. He wasn't being pushed towards climax this time, it was as if he was being suspended in a perfect state of being, those few seconds when one absolutely knew orgasm was coming, but before it took over the whole body.

Darric was still speaking, but Aden could no longer hear the words. It was as if his skin was being whispered to, every syllable a caress, every word a perfect expression of desire. A finger—sweeping, teasing, filling him up until he wanted more. The bed rocked as Blaze moved and angled himself over Aden.

Aden arched as Blaze touched something inside him, and stars burst behind his eyelids. "Blaze," Aden whined breathlessly, needing something but not knowing what.

"Shh." Darric kissed his lips, but Aden couldn't stay still.

"More, please." Aden wrenched his lips away and burned as he felt Blaze's fingers easing into his tight hole. Conner mouthed the soft skin underneath his cock; he could nearly feel the blood pound through him under Conner's tongue. Aden shifted restlessly, he was suddenly baking hot. He shivered.

"The bond has started to form. We need to complete. He's burning up." Darric murmured.

The touch of cool hands was so good on his hot skin, but he moaned for more. He needed so badly, something that was just out of his grasp; he arched in protest.

"Shh...baby, we've got you."

Aden murmured incoherently, he ached so badly. He needed Blaze.

Blaze read his thoughts, pressing his hot lips against Aden's. Oh, so right. So perfect. Other hands danced on his skin, teasing, feathering, driving him out of his mind.

"It is time." Aden vaguely heard Darric, but as if he were a million miles away.

"Beautiful Aden." Aden nearly cried at the sound of Conner's voice as Conner fastened his lips around his aching nipples.

"Please. Please." Aden was begging, and he didn't know for what. His skin was on fire. He needed—

"I'm here. Try to relax, sweetheart." Blaze's words grounded him a little. He was aware of the soft click of the lube bottle, and a wonderful, brief cooling feeling under his balls. He felt an arm reach around the backs of his legs, lift them and draw them upwards. Aden was panting. It was if he was thundering towards something, something incredibly important. Something he needed so desperately.

He felt Blaze's finger move so slowly, and he reached down to grab his aching cock, but Darric beat him to it. Conner's lips caught his mouth and swallowed every needy gasp until Aden was spinning in sensation. He felt a second finger, the pain suddenly intense.

"He's not relaxing," Blaze gasped the words out. "I'm going to hurt him."

"Let me." Darric lifted himself up from the bed and palmed Aden's face around to him. "Aden. Gorgeous boy. Look at me." Aden whined and thrashed his head, all and any concentration impossible. "Aden, look at me."

Finally, Aden took a breath and when he did, he seemed to fall headlong into Darric's deep, gray eyes. He blinked, and took another breath.

"That's it. Just keep looking at me. Feel how our hearts beat as one?" Darric lifted Aden's fisted hand and enclosed it in his own, over his heart.

"All yours, Aden. All yours forever."

He tried to turn towards the pain, tried to look at Blaze.

"Aden, stay with me. Just here." Darric wouldn't let go of Aden's face, so Aden refocused on those beautiful eyes. "Just look at me and relax. Think about how good it feels. How much you want this."

Oh God, yes he did. So, so much. He breathed in and out again with Darric. Aden's lips parted. He was going out of his mind. He needed Blaze, needed him.

He saw Darric's soft smile and heard the pleasure in his mind from all of them. "Breathe with me." Aden dissolved under Darric's calm words. He was ready for this. He felt more lube plastered around his tight hole as Blaze eased in slowly. Aden moved restlessly. His lips parted on a cry as pain flared suddenly in his ass.

Blaze, please.

"Look at me Aden, keep looking at me." Darric brushed small kisses on Aden's lips, so gentle. He whimpered at the pain, but Darric was almost detaching him from it.

Blaze stopped inching and held still. Aden thought he would split in two. *There's no way.* He wrenched his eyes from Darric and looked at Blaze, ready to shout. Blaze was poised, completely still. Every tendon stood out on his neck from the effort of not moving. Harsh gasps left his lips, and his eyes were screwed tightly shut. Blaze was barely hanging on by a thread.

Aden was awestruck that this powerful man cared so much about his comfort to discipline himself like this. Taking a slow breath and keeping his eyes firmly fixed on Blaze, Aden finally relaxed and slowly moved, swinging his hips a little, inviting Blaze deeper.

Blaze's eyes snapped open, and he slid in until his hips pressed against Aden's. Aden melted as a wide smile shone across the man's face—a smile he had put there. Aden arched as Darric's teeth found his nipple, and the gentle tug took his focus from the discomfort. Blaze inched again, and Conner tongued his cock. Pain and pleasure melded into one.

Darric caught his mouth and Aden was lost. It was impossible to feel this good. Long swipes from Conner's tongue had Aden ready to shoot again in seconds. Darric swallowed every warning moan, and Blaze slid out, then back in, time and time again until Aden was delirious with need. His mind swirled with unnamed emotions as his whole body tightened and thundered towards orgasm. Just as he reached the pinnacle of the hill, Conner pushed down and deep throated him. And that was what it took to launch him off the cliff. He barely heard Blaze shout with his own release.

He was floating somewhere, probably out of his body. He smiled at the thought, too exhausted to care.

When he became aware again, he was gently curled up in Conner's arms, so tired. He barely had the strength to nuzzle Conner's neck, but cracked an eye open in time to see Darric devouring Blaze's mouth. It was beautiful.

Chapter Eight

ADEN DOZED, LYING ON Conner's chest, utterly content for the first time in his life. He was aware of three things. His heart was so full it was likely to burst. It was incredibly sexy listening to Blaze and Darric loving each other, while Conner was holding him tight, and he seriously doubted his dick would function for the next hundred years. He smiled as Conner's chest rumbled with laughter.

No, four—four things. He needed to go to the bathroom and winced. He may be unable to walk.

Then I will carry you, Conner said.

A harsh knock on the door startled everybody.

Blaze was up and pulling his pants on before Aden could blink. Darric quickly reached for the sheet and covered all three of them, but Blaze disappeared out of the door.

Darric bent his head to Aden's, and sighed. Aden lifted his lips to kiss Darric in shared disappointment, and smoothed his fingers through Conner's hair. He smiled and sent a thought out. *I have over six hundred years to catch up on. We have time.*

Darric shook his head. *We didn't finish.* Aden looked in sympathy; he'd seen Blaze and Conner together.

Conner leaned over and kissed Aden's mouth. *He didn't mean that.*

Aden eyed them both.

Conner nibbled Aden's bottom lip. *To complete the bonding, you also take Blaze.*

Aden's mouth dropped open in astonishment and disbelief, as Blaze came back into the bedroom.

Aden felt the concern radiating from him. "What is it?"

"Do you know a Kellan?"

Aden sat up, startled. "From my old pack. He's Jay's older brother. His family was always good to me."

Aden caught the look Blaze shared with Conner and Darric. "What is it?"

Blaze went to one of the doors leading from the other side of the bedroom, next to the bathroom. *You need to get dressed, little one.*

Aden gingerly got out of bed. The room was awash with feelings of frustration, distaste, and—Aden turned his head to Conner—jealousy. Conner blushed. Aden shook his head in utter disbelief, and Darric growled, getting out of bed and reached for his jeans. "I do not like this, Blaze. I smell deceit."

Darric frowned and Aden heard a gasp from Conner. "Absolutely not."

He swung his head to Blaze as he appeared back from the room holding some soft sweats and a polo shirt. "What's wrong?"

Blaze handed the clothes to Aden. "He is insisting he sees you on your own."

Aden was surprised, but as he carefully got out of bed he said. "I'm not surprised, really. You three can be incredibly intimidating." He tried to smile reassuringly at Conner particularly. Distress was just pouring off the guy. He pulled his shirt down and reached for Conner's hand. In a flash, he stood beside him.

"Let me go to the bathroom first." Aden winced again. His ass still hurt, but he felt branded, stamped, as if he knew who he belonged to. He went to the bathroom and cleaned himself up quickly. He was trying not to think of the last thing Conner had said before Blaze had come back in.

"We can't let him go in there alone, Blaze," Darric insisted.

Blaze nodded. "We all go in there. I want to meet this man. If we are then satisfied with Aden's safety, we will wait outside."

Darric growled annoyance, but a look from Blaze silenced him instantly. "He is not a prisoner, Darric. He comes to us of his own free will or not at all."

Even Aden was impressed at that, and he followed Blaze to the door. At the last second he reached out and caught Conner's hand. He felt the tension bleed out of the guy. He could still feel his worry, but at least the brown eyes smiled a little. "I am sorry. It is just you are so important to me." *To us.* Darius echoed the thought.

"Then let's go see what the problem is." Aden wished he felt as confident as he sounded. Then he wanted to kick himself, as he heard the low, protective growls of his mates. Of course they heard his thoughts.

Maybe he needed a mute button?

He heard more soft growls behind him and smiled.

Instead of heading to the large meeting room where they had seen the Senator, Blaze turned in the opposite direction. Aden still clasping Conner's hand, following. He glanced down at their entwined fingers. It was odd, he didn't feel childish or stupid, just incredibly lucky. The hand squeezed his in answer. Aden walked calmly down the wide corridor. He knew they must be near the kitchen as the delicious smells were making his stomach growl. He patted his stomach idly with the hand that wasn't clasped in Conner's, and remembered Darric telling him he would look cute with a pot belly.

Before he could finish the thought, Blaze turned and they came face to face with a closed door. Two huge men Aden hadn't seen before stood on either side like sentinels. They both inclined their heads in deference as Aden, Conner, and Darric followed Blaze into the room.

Aden gasped in shock. Kellan sat on a chair next to a table with a jug of water and a tray of glasses in the center, but Aden was more concerned with the blood he could see on Kellan's face. He let go of Conner to hurry forward, only to be blocked by Darric.

Aden turned slightly irritated eyes on Darric. "Really?" He gestured to the man slumped in the chair being tended gently by an older man with gray hair. Aden assumed he was a pack doctor or healer.

Kellan lifted his battered and swollen face to Aden's. "Dear God, Kellan." Aden was horrified. "Who did this?" Kellan just clamped his lips and glared defiantly at Blaze.

Aden turned to Blaze. "He won't hurt me."

"We will just be outside." Blaze touched Aden's arm lightly and Aden felt a wave of comfort wash over him. Then he hesitated, and looked at Aden. *We will respect your privacy, and I will shut down our link.* Blaze's lips tilted up a fraction. *You can have your mute button, but please don't be long, little one.*

Aden nodded, and watched everyone including the doctor leave. "Kellan, do you need a drink?" Aden poured some water and offered it to the man. Kellan's hands shook, so Aden kept hold of the glass. Kellan hissed slightly as the water passed his cut lips.

"You want to tell me what happened?"

Kellan winced as he touched his face. "I've been sent to convince you to return." Aden's eyebrows rose in disbelief, and Kellan tried to nod. "I know, I've seen your new bodyguards."

"But why, Kellan?" Aden felt the distress emanating from the man.

"They have Jay."

Aden blindly reached for the chair, his legs threatening to give way. His heart hammering in his chest. "Jay? Who has Jay?" Although he knew the answer even as he said it.

"Alpha Craig and his enforcers." Kellan leaned forward, the tears plain in his usually dry eyes. "They're gonna torture him until you come back."

Aden's heart banged against his ribs, and he was suddenly glad that Blaze had turned their connection off. All three guys would be looking for someone to kill right about now.

He thought about Jay, how he'd never given him one second's problem since Aden couldn't shift at fifteen, how he'd helped his parents hide him from the Alpha, how'd he shrugged and laughed when Aden had told him he was gay, and teased that he would always be his friend but Aden hadn't better get any other ideas.

"The second message," Kellan continued, "is that you come alone or Jay will be dead before you get there."

Aden shook his head in anguish. "But that's impossible, they're—" Aden cut off the word *powerful*. He also didn't say they would be able to tell what he was feeling, thinking. "I don't know how to get out of here without them. Apart from my mates, there are wolves all over the place."

Kellan glanced at him, surprised. "You'll come?"

Aden touched his arm without thinking, and Kellan calmed visibly. "Of course I'll come. How could I not?"

"Mates? They're your mates?" Incredulity wove its way through Kellan's words. "I thought omegas—"

"Couldn't have mates?" Aden finished the question. "A lot of what we were told was wrong." Aden bit his lip. "I just have no way of getting out of here without them knowing."

Kellan winced as he stood. "This is all mixed up. I-I can't ask this of you."

"You have no choice, Kellan, It's not that I'm a prisoner, but they will know." Aden nearly cried in disbelief. He was talking like he intended to go with Kellan.

Kellan nodded, then he stilled. "I almost forgot. My mother? She gave me something. She said it would mask your scent if you chose to return. She said it wouldn't work for very long." Kellan flushed a little, mumbling the last line. "She never got a chance to tell me any more before the betas made me leave. They roughed me up so I wouldn't get any ideas about challenging them."

Aden watched as Kellan fished around in his pocket. "What is it?" He was curious because Jay's mom had experimented with herbs for a long time.

A lot of wolves chose to have her treat their injuries.

"They checked me for weapons, but they weren't interested in anything else." Kellan carefully opened a small folded up piece of paper. A small amount of white powder clung to the inside. He turned and slid it into a glass and topped it up with water. "Mom said it's for protection, or something." Kellan swallowed. "I'm sorry, that could be a load of shit. I have no idea what this stuff is. Mom could be talking nonsense, but she wouldn't give me anything that would hurt you."

Aden picked the glass up. He trusted Jay's mom, and he knew he would have seconds before his mates would be ready to barge back in. The five minutes Darric had grieved about giving Aden were already over. Aden clutched the glass tighter to stop his hand from shaking.

Jay. Jay was his best friend. The thought of going with Kellan was terrifying, but he knew that his Alphas would find him again. If he could just get to Jay, and give them enough time to find him, everything would be all right. He had no choice anyway, he couldn't be responsible for putting someone else through the nightmare he had suffered, and there was no way any of his Alphas would agree to let him go. Jay could be seriously hurt by then. Before he had a chance to second guess himself, Aden tipped the contents down his throat.

Almost immediately a feeling of calm washed over him and he stumbled as his legs wobbled. Kellan stood and took the glass before he dropped it, murmuring soothing words that Aden couldn't quite hear. Aden's vision darkened and Kellan's strong arms supported him. For a second he thought he was going to pass out.

When his vision righted itself he was sitting on Kellan's lap. That was odd. He shook his head, confused. That was—no, not odd—it was wonderful. Aden raised his eyes in wonder at the gorgeous smiling face that stared back at him. Kellan. If he was honest, Aden had fantasized over him for years. Aden ran his hands up the muscled arms and reveled in the deep chuckle coming from the man's strong chest.

"So, Ade. How you feeling now?"

Aden blushed. *Ade*. Kellan had a nickname for him, how—God, that was so special. Aden licked his lips and leaned into Kellan's chest. Hot sensations rushed through him, and he whimpered as he felt the hand that was stroking his leg. Kellan, how could he have forgotten? He'd dreamed about him for so long, never dared imagine he would ever touch him.

"We have to leave." Kellan moved his head just as Aden thought he was going to kiss him. Aden nearly cried in frustration.

The door opened quickly and three huge guys barreled into the room. Aden turned back, annoyed at the interruption; they had no business spoiling his time with Kellan.

He ignored the gasps from the three men that had barreled into the room, and gently threaded his fingers through the hairs on Kellan's chest that were just peeking out of his t-shirt. Aden nearly melted when Kellan's hand covered his own protectively. He whined softly, his body thrumming with the need to get closer.

"Aden?"

He turned, annoyed. The man with black hair looked angry, his blue eyes glittering. He had no idea why this big guy was still talking when he wanted to be left alone with Kellan. Kellan stood up and Aden gasped as Kellan slid his body to the floor. He hung on and ground his cock desperately into Kellan's leg. Just a little nearer.

"Aden?" The tortured tone got his attention then. Aden frowned at the man with brown eyes.

Kellan tucked him into his side. "I want to return with my mate."

Aden vaguely heard other gasps, but he didn't take any notice. He was too busy recovering from the words he had waited all his life to hear. Mate. Kellan's mate. It was perfect. "Yes, we need to go," he said. They had a life to start together.

"Aden? Is this true?"

Aden looked at the blazing blue eyes and a sudden memory pushed in. He'd told Aden something about him staying here. Yes, that was it. "You said it was my choice to stay here. That you would never force me." He glanced at the swimming brown eyes of the fair-headed guy, and nearly cringed when the guy with the blue eyes fisted his hands. Something was really making him angry.

Aden had to convince them. He put his hand up to Kellan's face. "I've always loved Kellan, I just never thought he was interested."

Kellan's eyes burned into Aden's face, and he held onto him tight. "You heard him. You have to let us go."

The one with the silver hair flashed angry gray eyes and took a hurried step forward. Aden cringed, suddenly scared. That halted all of them. The man immediately looked horrified. "Aden." He nearly choked the word out. "I would never."

The fair-haired man seemed to crumple in on himself and Aden peered confused as the blue-eyed one put his arm around him to support him. Aden felt uncomfortable, and shook his head slightly. He didn't want to upset anyone.

"My love?" Aden turned at Kellan's words and his discomfort lifted instantly. He lifted his lips invitingly, but Kellan chuckled and Aden pouted in annoyance.

"When we get home, sweetheart."

The one with the black hair stepped forward again. "How do we know he will be unharmed? Without proof, he will not be allowed to leave for his own protection, whether you are mates or not. He has been kept in appalling conditions for months. Where were you then?"

Aden felt Kellan stiffen. He hurriedly patted his mate to soothe him. He couldn't have him getting upset. Even though the words were washing over him, he wasn't really processing what was being said. Every nerve ending he had was screaming at him to get nearer to Kellan. He needed Kellan. He loved Kellan. That thought nearly forced a whimper from his lips once more.

Kellan hoisted him close once more. "Craig isn't like the old Alpha. Things will change in the pack. I was never one of the inner circle, there was nothing I could do."

The black haired giant opened his mouth to speak, but then paused. Aden blinked confused. He'd seemed so angry, now he just seemed so sad, defeated.

Aden didn't understand why that felt wrong. "We will visit to make sure you keep your word about his safety."

Aden just wanted to go. He wanted to be with Kellan, and all this talking was making his head spin. He couldn't concentrate on anything.

Kellan started walking Aden to the door, holding him tight, which was really nice because his legs felt a little numb and he wasn't sure how effective they would be.

"Aden." The breathless word came from the guy with the fair hair and brown eyes. "This is what you want? No one is forcing you? You officially reject us as mates?"

The silver haired guy blurted out, "Aden, you will no longer hear us, or we you."

Aden barely glanced at either of them. Why would he want to hear their nonsense? He fixed his eyes on Kellan, the one person that his heart beat for. "Yes. I never realized how much I love you, Kellan." Kellan's eyes shone triumphantly and practically carried Aden to the door. He vaguely heard a harsh cry as the dark-haired guy let the blond collapse on him, as if he couldn't take his own weight.

Aden barely noticed the short drive to the gates. He was unaware of people talking and laughing as he was bundled into another vehicle. He wanted to sit next to Kellan and was frustrated when Kellan sat in the front next to the driver. Someone was talking to him, trying to get his attention, and he turned sharply and saw a man with green, assessing eyes. Aden shook slightly, and something familiar skittered up his spine—a memory—but he couldn't quite fix on it. He reached his hand out to touch Kellan, but the man slapped his arm away.

"K-Kellan?" he hugged his arm, didn't understand why Kellan wouldn't touch him. Why he was suddenly being like this.

Kellan turned around in his seat and Aden's stomach dropped at the hatred and contempt he saw in his gaze. "Dirty little fag. Do you know how much trouble you've caused my family?" Kellan shook his head in disgust. "You make my skin crawl just looking at you. You've never cared about Jay, and he stood by you for years."

Aden could nearly hear the sound of his own heart breaking and the anguished tears that rolled down his face burned a track on his skin. He shook his head, trying to clear his thoughts, but as he did he felt the man beside him push his sleeve up roughly. Aden didn't realize what the man was going to do until he felt the sharp sting of a needle, and glanced down in shock at a syringe.

The man with the green eyes leaned into Aden's body and whispered. "Welcome home, little omega, there's a nice cage with your name on it waiting for you."

He dimly heard the others in the car laugh as he felt the numbness in his arm spread like fire to the rest of him. He had a second to realize something was really wrong, until everything went black.

He was so cold. Aden moved restlessly, wanting Blaze or Conner. Darric, whose arms would wrap him so tightly and make him feel so safe. Where were they?

He inhaled, and terror struck him along with a familiar stench. He barely had a second to register the smell and where he was when what seemed like gallons of cold water were flung at him. Gasping, choking, and coughing he reared up, only to bang his head on steel bars. The shock and the cold opened his eyes, and he froze. He was staring right into the cruel green ones of the person he hated the most.

Aden shrank back to the back of the cage, shaking so much, buck naked and shivering, so cold his mouth could hardly form words. "Why?"

He heard a laugh and saw Alpha Craig standing next to the pack doctor, Gregory Madden, smirking. "You're sure that stuff will mean they can't find him?"

"Yes, Alpha. It will be as if he disappeared from the planet." Aden looked horrified as he saw the doctor reach over to the table and pick up a syringe—just like the one he had given him earlier.

"It wouldn't matter anyway, you should have seen their faces when the little fag said he loved me." Aden shook his head in disbelief as Kellan came into view. Memories slammed into him. How could he? What had they given him? Blaze's insistence that he was promised safety, Darric's utter anguish when Aden had shrunk back from him—as if Darric would ever lay a finger on him—and Conner, his lovely Conner. In that second, as he remembered Conner crumpling up with pain, Aden suddenly didn't care what they did to him, because nothing would be worse than reliving the seconds when he had hurt immeasurably the three people who were so precious to him.

Craig laughed as rough hands opened the cage and pulled him out. "So now what shall we do with you?" He turned to his guards. "A little sport maybe?" He laughed at Aden. "You had a few days' rest, let's see if you can run any faster this time."

Aden could hardly process what was being shouted to him, and he barely cared. Now that he was fully conscious, he was only aware of the heart-breaking desolation that surrounded him. He had rejected them, his mates. He had caused incredible hurt to people who had done nothing but care for and protect him. Conner's face; that had been the worst. He would never forget how he had looked as he had left and how Blaze had had to catch him. All his memories returned. He had no idea what was in the powder, but he had obviously been tricked.

Blaze? Conner? Darric? Where are you? Aden could have cried in hopelessness. He remembered Darric's words as he'd rejected them. *You will no longer hear us, or we you.* He hadn't understood what that meant then, but he did now.

He was pushed forward by the Alpha and tripped. Unable to use his arms fast enough to steady himself, he went sprawling. He was yanked back up immediately, and came face to face with Kellan.

"Is Jay safe?" Aden asked.

Kellan opened his mouth to rain more hatred and contempt down on Aden, but as the words sank into Kellan, a surprised look crossed his face. It was gone in an instant. "Dirty fag," he spat out. "How dare you mention my brother."

Craig stepped back up, fairly salivating in anticipation. "Now run, little omega. Run if you know what's good for you." His words were nearly drowned out by the growls of the gammas that had appeared to surround him.

Panic beat at Aden's chest. He had to run.

Then suddenly even greater despair washed over him. His heart felt like it had been yanked from his body, and if the gammas weren't holding him, he would have sunk to the floor. His mates. They were gone. Every cell in his body screamed in pain, and his vision dimmed a little.

"What's the matter with him?" Kellan sounded nervous.

The doctor frowned. "Have any of you heard of the legend of Sirius's wolves?"

Kellan and a few of the gammas looked nervously at each other.

"That's bedtime stories for pups." The derision in Craig's voice was clear.

The doctor looked at Aden assessingly. "Actually, Alpha, that isn't totally certain anymore. There are recent rumors of an Alpha triad, and from what Kellan has told us, it seems to be bearing out."

Aden had sunk to the floor as the gammas were concentrating more on the doctor.

"What do you mean?" Kellan asked. He glanced at Aden. "There were three wolves with him. He said they were to mate but that's impossible."

"It is said that when the relationship between humans and wolf-shifters is at its worst, Orion's Circle will be formed to save mankind."

Craig scoffed. "Fairytales."

Gregory nodded. "Your father certainly thought so."

"And omegas don't mate," Kellan put in.

"Yes, that is true," Gregory said.

Even Aden wasn't so far gone that he didn't pick up on the slight hesitation from the doctor.

Craig either chose to ignore it or it went over his head. "Enough of this crap. Everyone's been feeling restless for days, we need a good hunt to get it out of our system." He pointed to Aden. "That's what the little faggot's for.

My father always told me, get an omega and the pack will be yours."

He rubbed his hands and nodded to the gammas. Aden was hoisted to his feet, every nerve in his body on edge. What was the point? He would never have his mates. He had hurt them so much they would never ever love him again. He remembered the conviction that they would come for him. Then he remembered Blaze's face as he had left, the utter devastation he had caused. Blaze wouldn't come for him now, none of them would.

Aden tried to balance as the gammas raised him, but instead of hanging his head and refusing to look at the Alpha as he had always done with Craig's father, Aden lifted his chin and stared at Craig. One word. "No."

The room went deathly quiet. Aden caught Kellan's slight wince.

"What the fuck did you just say to me?" Alpha Craig almost whispered the words in utter disbelief.

"I said no." Aden drew himself up taller. "I will not provide you with sport. Go ahead," he shot out the challenge. "Go ahead and kill me. Life without my mates is not worth a thing."

Aden didn't even brace as he saw Craig's fist hurling towards him. He stumbled and fell as agony bloomed across his face. He could taste the blood that exploded from his nose, and fell back, collapsing on the floor. He wouldn't run. He wouldn't protest. He just wanted death to come as fast as possible.

He blearily heard laughing as the gammas dragged him to his feet. Pain seared his face as harsh fingers grabbed his chin and pulled it around.

Craig smiled. "Who said anything about killing you?" Aden panted in dismay. Craig had been taught well by his father, but he looked like he had a few tricks of his own. "You would be amazed what a shifter body can put up with."

The doctor chuckled softly as if in agreement. "I think a beating would make you feel better, Alpha."

Craig nodded to one of the gammas, and Aden felt the first punch the man threw. By the time Craig added the fourth, Aden no longer felt his legs. After another few minutes, the pain was so great Aden was convinced the doctor was wrong. No one could stand this, no one. Finally, after the last punch sent his mind reeling towards the encroaching darkness, unconsciousness was a welcome relief as Aden's body shut down.

Chapter Nine

Aden barely felt the cold water that the gammas flung at him this time.

Hot needles tore at his flesh when rough hands dragged him out of the cage. He thought this was the fifth day this had happened, but he couldn't be sure. Every day Craig tried to get him to run, and every day he'd refused. He hadn't been given any food, but he wasn't hungry anyway. He whimpered…how much longer? How much longer would he have to suffer?

"Ade."

Aden's eyes opened in protest at the familiar voice. "J-Jay?"

"I—"

Jay's words were cut off by the gamma clamping a hand roughly over his mouth. Aden glanced around, panicked. Craig stood there with his arms folded and a triumphant smirk on his face. The doctor stood next to him observing quietly. There was no sign of Kellan.

Craig stepped forward, and he nodded to the gamma holding Jay. "As you refuse to run and give us any sport, you give us no choice but to make him take your place. Of course, as he is now essentially you, he will receive any punishment you would be due too, if you don't give us the sport we ask for." Sharp pain tore at Aden's scalp as Craig dragged his head up by his hair. "You are nothing. You are omega, the lowest of the low. This is all you are good for." Craig inhaled and spat at Aden. He didn't even have a free hand to wipe away the glob that landed across his cheek.

Aden looked helplessly, the sounds of Jay struggling echoing around the room. He nodded and opened his mouth.

"Ade, no. Don't—" Jay's words were cut off by the blow from the gamma.

Aden looked at the Alpha in complete resignation, and Craig smirked. He didn't need Aden to vocalize his surrender. Aden knew defeat was visible in the slump of his shoulders. Another sharp pain tore at his insides, and Aden knew this wasn't from his injuries. Blaze had warned him he would be sick without them there, and he knew it would be nearly impossible to run.

The doctor stepped forward and shot something painful into Aden's arm. He held something that looked like a gun. "That's so you don't get any ideas about wandering away from us too far." Aden looked at the red mark that dribbled a little blood. "It's a tracker, and the mark is now in your system. It is immovable."

The doctor turned back with a syringe. He smiled almost benevolently at Aden. "This is to mask the pain from your injuries. You can't run if you can't walk." Aden shook his head in disbelief. They wanted just to mask the pain, not actually give him anything that would heal him.

"Go," Craig said, "we don't care where. You get an hour's start."

Aden stumbled as the Alpha pushed him, uncaring. He took an agonized look at Jay, who was watching horrified as the gammas still held him, then lifted his chin. He had failed everyone, but at least he could protect Jay. They wanted sport? He would give them it.

Finding his legs not as shaky, whatever drug he had been given seeming to mask his hurts, Aden ran towards the door and down the steps. He squinted in the sunlight. Where the hell should he go?

He'd always headed for the forest before. There was nowhere to hide by the cluster of cottages, and he didn't want to risk anyone he knew being witness to his humiliation. He could hear a dog barking in the distance, the sounds of a motor being started. Aden sighed—he had no choice—so he picked his way around the trees. After alternating between running and walking for a while, and finding a stream where he could gulp some water, he realized he was nearing the edge of the woods and wasn't sure where he was, he'd never come this far away from camp before. He sat on a log desolately and winced as he picked some rough stones out from under his bare feet. He rubbed at his arm. He had no chance with the tracker; they only had to check where he was to hunt him.

He threw a stone at the stream in frustration; he was screwed all round, and the pain in his ribs and his face was coming back. His mind slid to somewhere else for a few seconds and the constant longing that was there, just waiting for him. He stood up. There was no way out of this.

Aden hovered, uncertain. This would be a cycle. Every time they wanted sport, Jay would be used to threaten him. If they didn't use Jay, there would be another. He couldn't live like this, just accepting daily beatings, accepting his life for what it was.

He needed this to be over, and Aden straightened as the solution suddenly stared him in the face. He had hoped for a few hours that he had another purpose in life, but that had been snuffed out because of his own stupidity. He had no doubt they would find another omega to complete their circle. Blaze had called him Psi, but he wasn't that special. He thought the three Alphas were the special ones. He wasn't clever or particularly brave. He'd cowered in that cage. Burning crept into his face as he realized he'd never tried hard to fight back after the first few days. He'd been pathetic. Yes, the gammas were bigger than him, but he'd never even tried...

Aden raised his face to the sun. At least it was warm—no one had bothered giving him any clothes—but this was shifter land. No one cared, and it was unlikely anyone would be around here. Aden dropped his head. He knew he was stalling, had already made his decision. He knew they would call him a coward, but he'd never thought what an incredible amount of courage it was actually going to take. He clinically thought over his options, and decided to look for something sharp. The things that had cut into his feet wouldn't work the same on his wrist, and he didn't have much time. He wasn't going back. He had glimpsed a perfect existence for two days; if he couldn't have that, he didn't want anything.

Aden trudged for a little while longer until he came to what he assumed was some sort of old property line. It had been marked out at some point because there were fence posts sticking out, and what looked to be a broken down old shed. There were some low stone walls that looked like the work of someone who once had tried to build some sort of house, but the idea had been abandoned a long time ago. Aden walked over quickly in case there was anything he could use...he swallowed. *A tool. Anything sharp.*

Just as he approached, a faint howl echoed from the trees, and every hair on Aden's body stood up. Fear skittered down his spine. It was Craig and the gammas, they knew where he was. Frantically, he looked at the fence post in front of him. There wasn't even any wire.

Time seemed to stand still. His heart pounded so fast it could have escaped his chest. He gazed at a jagged, rusty spike pointing out of the wood. He'd nearly missed it because it was so rusty that the brown of the wood masked it.

Aden reached quickly with both hands and tugged. The wood behind was rotten, so it came out easily. He heard another howl, nearer; he had barely a few minutes. Aden spied a thicket between two trees and he pushed into the space, ignoring the sharp thorns that grazed him. He lifted the spike up. Should he go for his heart? No, that was ridiculous, it wasn't long enough. It would have to be his wrist. Aden swallowed, his hand shaking so badly he was worried he wouldn't find the courage he needed.

Aden.

It was Conner's voice. Aden felt such an immense wave of gratitude wash over him that his mind in his last moments—when his courage was deserting him—had produced the exact thing he needed. He pressed the spike into his wrist and saw the blood bloom underneath on his skin. He didn't even feel the pain. His mind was being stroked by the word his imagination had just whispered to him. Held, comforted. Everything was going to be all right. He pushed the spike in further and watched with fascination as the blood spurted. He swapped the spike into his other hand, the blood making his fingers slippery.

Aden stop. Wait.

Aden hesitated. That had sounded real. Tears welled in his eyes as he wished again for the impossible, but shouts and growls tore his mind away and, panicked, he pressed the spike firmly into his other wrist, and drew it across.

After the fourth time they'd brought him around with more cold water, Aden didn't even try to crawl away. He couldn't believe they had pulled him out of that thicket. Another minute and his suffering would have been over. His stupid imagination had teased him with Conner's voice and he had hesitated just too long to finish himself off before the pack had found him. His days had melded into one long period of agony. He was detached almost from the beatings, thankfully, and his mind had taken him to a place where it almost didn't hurt anymore.

He had no idea what amount of time had passed. He'd half come awake earlier to realize he lay in his own piss. The disgust horrified him even more than the earlier pain. If he tried very hard he could almost imagine the soft touches of Conner and the subtle teasing visions from Darric. How Blaze would stand and protect him. He zoned out the shouts and the noise, and drifted down into his dream. At least there he was safe. No one could hurt him there.

He came to, bleary, realizing the gammas were holding him up outside the cage. The doctor and the Alpha were talking in quick, hushed tones.

"There is a chance they may not want him."

Craig scoffed in complete derision. "How would they not want him? Of course they mean to steal my omega." He laughed hysterically. "They're all fucking fags. It makes me want to vomit when I think of what they will do." Aden never attempted to say a word. A faint stirring of hope drizzled through him. Were his mates finally coming for him? His head lolled back on his shoulders, he was so tired. It hurt to think, everything hurt.

"That does seem to be the problem, Alpha." Gregory screwed his face up as if in concentration. Aden was starting to zone out again, and he struggled to focus on what was being said. He wanted to hear what they were saying but he couldn't concentrate. He was so thirsty, and so tired.

"Of course, if he was no good to them physically, that might be a suitable deterrent." Aden heard the quiet words as if a bomb had dropped in the room. He struggled, complete panic giving him strength at the gleam in the Alpha's eyes.

Craig crowed. "Perfect. He is still my omega and couldn't fuck anyone if he wanted." The Alpha leaned his head back and laughed delightedly. "Get me a knife," he shouted to his gammas.

Aden didn't know how he was still conscious. The paralytic fear that had washed over him at the Alpha's words had sent his mind reeling.

"Get me a knife," screamed the Alpha as shouts and screams sounded outside the doors, but the gammas holding Aden panicked and let him drop to the floor.

Aden frantically tried to stand, until Craig pulled him up again.

"Imbeciles," he shouted at the gammas, and they rushed to pick Aden up again, holding him in front of the Alpha.

Aden could hear the sound of fighting. His heart leapt at the noise; this was why the gammas were panicking.

Blaze. He was coming for him.

Craig shot a worried glance at the door. "Anything," he beckoned frantically with his hand, "quickly."

Aden was desperate. He could hear the shouts and the sounds of struggle, and they were getting louder and nearer. Craig glanced around the room. "Someone get me a fucking knife," he screamed in fury, as wolves started to stream into the room.

The doctor pulled a small bottle out of his bag. "Quick, this will have to do, it burns."

Aden struggled in the arms that clamped him tightly until he met the Alpha's eyes. Then, it seemed like the world stopped, and the sounds of the fighting fell away. He'd thought he was used to contempt, used to the violence that his life had become, but the look of utter hatred in the Alpha's eyes took his breath away. For a few seconds he didn't feel fear, just complete and overwhelming pity that any being, human or wolf, could exist with such blackness in his heart. It was wrong.

The door slammed open with an almighty crash, but that was when the hate in Craig's eyes turned to triumph as he threw the contents of the vial at Aden's groin.

At the same second that the gammas dropped him where he stood and jumped away in fear, Aden doubled up as excruciating pain hit his skin. The blackness that thundered toward him thankfully robbed him of any coherent thought.

Harsh sounds and someone's urgent hands were tugging on him. He whimpered in protest. He just wanted to lay there and drift, but there was so much noise. Aden tried to close his mind to the noise, shut off the impossible breathtaking pain. Someone was even calling his name. Hands lifted him and a harsh whine tore from his throat. Why couldn't they just leave him alone to die?

"Aden. Aden, listen to me. We have to move you."

Aden screwed his eyes up against the words. He knew it wasn't Blaze. If it was, he would have called him—*Little one.*

Chapter Ten

Aden drifted. He wasn't sure whether he was alive or dead. Pain so fierce he thought he would go mad plagued every second of his existence. He thrashed, his skin so hot he thought the very flames of hell lapped at him. His mind kept teasing him with voices—Darric often, sometimes Blaze, sometimes both of them. Hushed, worried, like he was already dead.

Aden climbed slowly out of his nightmare. He remembered the blinding pain and wretched agony, and whimpered in protest. He tried to open his glued eyes and blinked. The smell hit him instantly and he turned.

Blaze.

"B-Blaze?" his mouth was so dry he could hardly get the words out. Another hand reached around his head and Aden recoiled in shock.

"Now, now, Aden, just getting you some water, nothing to fear." Aden gaped as a woman smiled and held out a glass of water. He shot a look at Blaze, but Blaze just nodded. "Drink it, Aden."

It was a good job the woman kept hold of the glass because Aden's hand was shaking so much he couldn't hold it.

"Alpha, would you like me to help the omega bathe?"

Aden choked on the rest of the water at that sentence. The woman clucked and shushed him as she took the glass away. Aden looked at Blaze, his tongue tying itself in all sorts of knots. He didn't understand why Blaze sat at such a distance from him, nor where Conner and Darric were. Blaze shook his head. "No, Debbie, thank you. You may go." The woman stood, still smiling kindly at Aden, then left the room.

Aden shook his head in disbelief. "Tell me I'm not dreaming." As soon as the woman was out of the room, he nearly cried in gratitude and moved, intending to get as close as possible to where Blaze was. The clang of chains on his wrists pulled him up short. Aden stared down at his manacled wrists in disbelief. "B-Blaze?"

Blaze stood up from his position in the corner. "It is a precaution so you don't wander off. Your pack, Black Lakes, is disbanded. Jefferson's Alpha has put in a team to manage while it is decided what to do. Alpha Craig and his betas are dead. Darric healed your injuries as before, as best he could."

At Blaze's hesitation, memory rushed in and Aden paled. "W-what?" Aden stammered in disbelief. He scrambled to pull at his shorts and the sight nearly made him sick. Rows of puckered, scarred flesh in long red lines started at his abdomen and streaked across his cock and balls. Two of them stretched to the top of his thighs. Aden gaped in shock.

"As I said, as best he could. The acid was designed to destroy quickly, and he was not with me at your compound."

Aden heard Blaze's words as if the man were speaking from a long distance away.

"You are not in any pain?"

Aden shook his head miserably. At least that was something. He traced the biggest scar with his finger, one that ran nearly the full length of his cock, and stopped. It wasn't that it didn't hurt, it was that he couldn't feel the skin at all.

"I can't." Aden's tongue wouldn't work. Embarrassment warred with fear.

Blaze looked coldly at Aden. "You're alive. I'm sure if there's a problem, you and your mate will adapt."

Aden's mouth gaped in shock. "B-but Blaze, he's not my mate. He—"

Blaze headed towards the door, as if Aden hadn't spoken. "You will be held here until you are recovered, then you may take your pick of packs to live in. Transport will be provided. Your mate is tethered downstairs. Much as I would have liked the satisfaction, he has been spared. He will remain a prisoner until you both leave."

Aden shrank when Blaze turned. Anger suffused the man's features, but as Aden watched, he pulled his face into a blank mask. "You deserve far worse for what you have put Conner through. I thought we would lose him three nights ago." Blaze raked contemptuous eyes over Aden. "It is only because you were beaten nearly to death, and now will be permanently scarred. We consider that punishment sufficient. There are plenty of packs in need of an omega. I am sure you will be of some use."

Aden shook his head, desperation making his words clumsy. "I didn't know—I mean, he isn't. They gave me something." His words trickled to a halt in front of the mask that Blaze wore. Why was he protesting? He deserved this. He had hurt them all so terribly. The drug may have made him say the words but it was his idiocy that made him drink it in the first place. Aden hung his head, then he processed what Blaze had said. "Conner? He's?"

"He will live, I think only because apart from when he was healing you, Darric hasn't left his side."

"But," Aden stammered, "how?" *Is he sick*, he wanted to ask, but the words died in his throat.

Blaze put his hand on the door. For one second Aden thought he would turn back around, but his heart sank as Blaze pulled the handle and stepped out. Just before he closed the door, he looked at Aden, and Aden shivered at the ice in his blue gaze. "Conner is possibly the most powerful empath on the planet, all emotions he feels are exponentially magnified. You were to mate. When you rejected him, we thought he would die of a broken heart." Aden gazed in horror at Blaze.

"I think it was only that you weren't fully bonded that Darric could save him."

Aden blinked and Blaze firmly closed the door.

Blaze's gammas had untied him twice to take him to the bathroom, and he had had trays full of food brought in and out of the room constantly. The gammas frowned as they returned each one untouched. He hadn't even been able to stomach water. He curled up, untouched and unloved. He didn't even cry, he had no strength left to do even that. He just wanted to die.

He felt the bed dip, and ignored it. The gammas would be changing the tray, untouched again.

He felt a hand brush his arm, and shied from the contact. He tried to unglue his dry tongue to speak. "No, please. Just leave me alone."

"But you don't want that, do you?"

Aden gasped as he opened his eyes to Darric. Even as his heart cried out to see him, he shrank back from Darric's touch. They just wanted to be cruel now, to know he suffered as much as he had made them suffer. Well, he deserved it. He tried to pull back some more, the chains stopping him move.

"This is ridiculous." Aden heard Darric curse, and the manacles dropped from his wrist. "Where in God's name does he think you're going to go?"

Aden briefly struggled as he felt Darric's strong arms lifting him. "Darling, why? Why didn't you tell Blaze? I can feel your honesty."

Darric smothered him in kisses and Aden just lay there, convinced that Darric's touch and words were a lie.

"I am so sorry, Aden. You weren't conscious before when I came to heal you. I didn't know." He smoothed the brown hair that flopped listlessly over Aden's pale face. "The gammas were worried. They said you hadn't even drunk anything. I came to see if you were still sick. Here." Darric reached over for the glass of water and pushed it at Aden's lips. Aden swallowed quickly, then coughed and choked. "Sips, Aden. Go slowly."

He swallowed some of the cool water and it tasted heavenly. He sighed, still afraid to move any further away from the warmth of Darric's embrace. "Conner?"

Darric smiled and pushed some more hair out of his eyes. "He's very weak. Blaze is staying with him while I come in here. I'm sorry you suffered needlessly. If Conner had been here, he would have known you were truthful straightaway."

Aden blinked slowly at Darric. "It wasn't your fault, I was so stupid. They had Jay." *Blaze.* "Darric? He hates me." Aden felt the thud of his useless heart as the truth pounded him.

"I have never seen Blaze so angry. He has fought to keep us safe for so long, and there was a real danger to Conner and there was nothing he could do. He felt powerless, and for an Alpha that's a big thing."

"He drugged me. Kellan." Aden raised imploring eyes to Darric. He had to believe him. "He told me the Alpha was torturing Jay until I returned. He said the drug would mask my scent and make it easier for you to let me go."

He heaved a shuddering breath. "He's not my mate."

Darric kissed his head. "I know. Blaze doesn't have Conner's gift of knowing when people are truthful, and rejecting us meant we cannot hear your thoughts. As soon as I entered the room I could feel your desire for love, for *our* love. Blaze could have looked, but he refused because he was convinced of your love for Kellan, and he didn't want to hear it."

Aden was still unsure. "You didn't see him when I woke up. He—" *He chained me.*

Darric smoothed his hair again. "And you didn't see him when he brought you back. He was beside himself, Aden. He blames himself for the condition you were in. If Conner hadn't been so sick, we would have checked on you days ago. I don't think he will ever forgive himself for that. It's his guilt that is making him lash out at you.

"Conner insisted you were hurt, that you were calling out to us through our link, but we could not hear you after Blaze turned it off, and Conner was delirious."

Aden brought his head up. "I need to see Conner." The thought of seeing Blaze petrified him, but he had to stop Conner's suffering, make sure he was okay. Conner *had* reached out. He had heard his voice despite what Blaze and Darric said. He would help Conner heal and then he would go—they would find another Psi to complete them. Aden shook again as that thought threatened to overpower him. He was no use to anyone now, not as a mate anyway. The last time Aden had been taken to the bathroom he had touched himself and he couldn't feel anything. It was a fitting punishment for what he had done.

"Hey." Darric lifted his chin and kissed away the fresh tears. "Come on, let's get this done." He shuffled to the edge of the bed and pulled Aden closer.

"No, Darric. I can walk."

Darric looked doubtful, but acquiesced. Somehow, it was important that Aden walked in there. He stood on shaky legs, and didn't complain at the large arm that held him upright. They shuffled out of the door. Aden wasn't exactly in pain, but he felt every step as if it was going to be his last one.

So, you can't hear me anymore? A wave of fresh tears broke over Aden when he didn't get a reply.

Darric frowned and brushed them away with his hand. "What is it?"

Aden shook his head. It was so lonely in his head without them all in there. Darric squeezed his hand gently and stopped at the door of the room they had all shared before.

"I can manage." Aden gently shook Darric's arm free. He wasn't sure he could, but he had to try. He tapped on the door and heard the low tone of Blaze bidding them to enter. Aden pushed the door open. Quick as a flash Darric stood in front of him protectively when Blaze moved so fast off the bed and with such fury, Aden thought he would kill him. But Blaze's angry voice and Darric's pleading faded away as soon as he saw the white face under the covers.

Conner looked like a ghost. Aden took one step, and couldn't help the anguished sob that broke free from him. Conner's eyes snapped open at the sound, and Aden nearly ran as those eyes widened incredulously.

"Aden?"

Then he was there, wrapped up and breathing in every part of Conner that was humanly possible. Aden cried, Conner cried, until his heart was so full he knew that was overflowing too.

After what seemed a lifetime, Aden was aware that everyone had suddenly become silent.

"It's true, Blaze," Darric said. "They drugged him. I knew he loved us as soon as I entered the room. It was because he was unconscious earlier that I didn't know."

"Aden."

Aden glanced back at Conner. The voice in the woods. He looked at his healed wrist. "It was you. I thought it was just in my head."

Conner smiled and laid his head back down, as if the small movement had exhausted him. "Of course it was me." He glanced at Blaze. "I didn't need the bond to hear him crying to us in pain." Conner gazed at him, his voice rough. "Never, ever think of doing that ever again."

Aden looked down. "I just couldn't do it anymore. If I hadn't heard your voice..." He heard the small, distressed noise from Darric, but didn't trust himself to look at him. Aden just clasped the fingers Conner reached out to him, carefully lying down and drawing the big man close. He could see Conner's eyes closing as much as he was valiantly trying to remain focused on Aden.

"Hush," Aden soothed. Conner heaved a huge sigh and settled his head in the crook of Aden's shoulder. Aden pushed the man's fair hair away from his closing, gentle brown eyes. "Go to sleep."

Conner didn't even reply. Aden waited for a few seconds until Conner was breathing deeply, then he carefully nudged him so he could get out without waking him.

"What are you doing?"

Aden shook. He didn't dare look. He could feel Blaze's blue eyes focusing on him, and if they were as full of ice and hatred as they had been before, he feared he would not live.

He felt the bed dip, and Aden raised his eyes.

"I didn't know," Blaze said quietly.

Aden cried at the sight of the big man's opened arms. He so desperately wanted to sink into them, but not now. It was too late.

Little one.

If Aden had any tears left, the sound of Blaze in his head would have made him weep again. Aden stood on shaky feet, ignoring the worried looks from Blaze and the frantic touches from Darric.

"You can get another omega to complete Orion's Circle, become the Psi you need."

"Sweetheart, we don't want another omega." Darric moved closer to him, and Aden took a hurried step back. He couldn't be Darric's focus, not now.

"I can't be your mate." Aden said shakily. "I can't be anyone's mate."

Blaze frowned. "What do you mean?"

"Aden, we didn't know you had been forced. Your rejection meant we couldn't see your thoughts." Darric tried to touch him, but Aden shrank back.

Darric made a small noise as if he were in pain. "Aden, is it your scars? We don't care about them."

Aden suddenly felt calm. The scent from Blaze seemed to fill him, and Aden knew what he was doing. He was searching Aden's thoughts. Aden never made any attempt to hide them. Blaze gasped and Aden sighed. At least he knew.

"It doesn't matter." Blaze was emphatic, but Aden didn't care. He was...less now, damaged. He knew it was the guilt controlling Blaze's feelings. When Blaze thought about it, he would feel relieved. Aden had always doubted he would be good enough for them, and now he knew he would never be.

Blaze stared steadily at Aden. "Please stay with Conner at least for now. You are as exhausted as he is. Everything else we will work out. You need rest and food. Everything else is unimportant for now." Darric looked puzzled at both of them.

Aden silently thanked Blaze for not telling Darric yet. He really wasn't ready for the insatiable sexual need that he couldn't do anything about.

Blaze shook his head slightly. "I'm sorry, Aden."

No pity. "Please stay out of my head now."

Darric gasped in shock at Aden's harsh words, and Blaze made a distressed sound and touched his arm. Aden just ignored it, shrugged Blaze's outstretched hand off, and climbed back into bed with Conner.

Chapter Eleven

A<small>DEN STILL WASN'T VERY</small> hungry, despite Blaze's urges and determination over the last few days to think up and provide every food stuff known to man. He'd picked uninterestedly at some fruit that seemed tasteless, ignoring frantic worried glances from Darric and the increasingly hard mask that Blaze wore.

Today, he'd awakened lying on his back. Darric lay curled up to one side and Conner had his head rested on Aden's abdomen. Aden was carding his fingers gently through Conner's hair. He felt the rumble from Darric, and was soothed by the soft even breaths from Conner.

"It's the first time he has properly slept in over a week." Blaze spoke quietly from where he was perched at the edge of the bed.

Aden jumped. He hadn't realized Blaze was there. As he looked up stricken, Blaze leaned over. "I'm sorry, that was thoughtless. We all suffered."

Aden desperately wanted Blaze's touch. "I don't understand why he got so sick," he said. "I thought you just had to shift to heal yourselves."

Blaze formed a wry smile. "It wasn't a physical injury, Aden. It was as if he just didn't want to live." Aden trembled. *Conner.*

Blaze continued. "Aden, I understand what you are worried about."

Aden felt his cheeks flame. His heart cried out in desperation, and Darric stirred.

Blaze leaned over and rested his hand on Aden's leg. "He feels your pain even as he sleeps. You are Psi. You complete us. We have waited for you for a long time. Scars are immaterial. This nonsense stops right now."

"But it's not just scars, I can't..." Aden wanted to curl up in despair. It was as if every time he had a chance at happiness, something took it away. He forced the words out. "We can't bond."

"Aden..." Blaze lifted his hand and Aden shrank. Blaze stopped himself reaching out for Aden. "We'll work it out. I want to stay, but I have other things to see to." Blaze ground the words out, and stood as if he didn't know what to do. Aden wanted to laugh hysterically. Blaze always knew what to do, this was completely unlike him.

Aden felt terribly guilty. He was just something else for Blaze to worry about. "You won't have had any sleep."

"I'm okay when my wolves are okay." Blaze looked at the door. "All of them."

Aden nodded. Taking down Black Lakes meant more things to sort out, apart from the meeting with the Defense Committee. "Did the meeting happen yet?"

"No, *lit*—Aden."

Aden nearly cried when he heard Blaze stop himself using Aden's nickname. *Little one.* He'd called him that from the beginning. Aden had resented it as it had made him feel childish, but now? He would do anything to hear it again.

Blaze took a step towards the door. He seemed reluctant to leave. "We managed to put them off for two days. We are due to start late tomorrow afternoon, and we all need to be there."

"Blaze?" Alarmed, something else occurred to Aden. "Jay? Is he all right, and Kellan—you have Kellan downstairs?"

"Conner made me go," the stark confession bled from Blaze. "He was delirious, but insisted I had to go. Insisted he had spoken to you, which I said was impossible. To my shame I rescued you for him more than for your sake." Blaze swallowed. "I will never forget what I saw when we entered your pack house. I was very nearly too late."

Aden's heart plummeted. His overbearing Alpha just felt immense guilt, not...*love*. Aden closed his eyes in despair. Blaze didn't love him; he was too caught up in everything he needed to do for others.

"We met Kellan in the woods close by," Blaze continued. "He insisted he was coming to tell us about you. I have not spoken to him since." Blaze paused. "Jay and the rest of your old pack are all okay. You will be able to see him when you are recovered."

Aden turned slightly as Darric's hand fell from his leg. He was asleep. At least Aden could bring comfort now, but not to Blaze. No, he would never—*could never*—mate with the Alpha.

Blaze sighed and walked out of the room.

Aden assumed it was around dawn the next time he woke. He'd smelled the three different scents immediately, and was just trying to decide how to get out of bed without waking anyone. Apart from the fact that he really didn't want a conversation with Blaze, if he didn't go to the bathroom soon, his bladder was going to burst. He tried easing his leg out from where it was pinned.

"Where you off to in such a hurry?" Blaze murmured, his voice full of sleep, just as Aden tried to reach his leg over Blaze to climb out, the edge of his limp, useless cock scraping against Blaze's naked body. Blaze's hands came out to clutch Aden closer to him.

Aden hung his head in shame. "Blaze, I need to pee."

Blaze's smile faltered and he seemed to come fully awake. He carefully deposited Aden on the side of the bed.

He managed to get to the bathroom under his own steam. He looked longingly at the shower, and glanced nervously at the door. He quickly strode back and clicked the lock. Aden shook his head at how pathetic his gesture was. *Like a flimsy piece of metal would keep any of them out.*

He turned the shower on and stepped inside. Aden closed his eyes at the sheer delight of warm water pounding his skin, and he soaped himself up quickly, keeping one ear out for the sound of the door opening.

He squeezed his eyes shut as he lowered his hand. His fingers traced the puckering of his scars. He yanked his hand away in disgust. He was horrible. A harsh sound echoed against the pounding of the water, and Aden was distraught to realize it was him who had made the noise.

He leaned back against the tiles in total despair. How could he do this? How, knowing that every day was just going to be worse than the one before? He turned off the water and stepped out, ignoring the full mirror on the wall. Aden listened carefully. There wasn't a sound from the bedroom—so much for locking the door. They were probably all thanking their lucky stars they didn't have to come in here. He dried himself quickly, couldn't bear to use the towel properly for his bottom half, and just skimmed it over his buttocks; then he wrapped it around his waist. He would have to go into the other room for clothes, but it didn't matter now, the others certainly had all left.

Aden unclicked the lock and yanked the door open a little more forcefully than he had to. He stepped out into the bedroom and came to an abrupt stop. *No, oh God, no.*

Darric lay on the bed, covers flung aside, completely naked. His gray eyes burned into Aden, and his long fingers were stroking his hard cock lazily.

Aden closed his eyes and his legs shook in desperation. It wasn't fair, why were they doing this? He snapped his eyes open in anger. "I can't, Darric. Is this a reminder of my stupidity? Is it? Is that what amuses you all? I said I will help while you get another omega. I can't *do* anything else." Aden nearly screamed the last line, barely aware that Darric had vaulted out of bed until he collapsed with a sob into big, strong arms that lifted him, a mouth that shushed him, and lips that bathed him in hot kisses.

Aden cried. Big, ugly tears. For the life he had lost as a child, for his parents, for the hell of the last year, and finally for the life he was now not going to have. Once the storm had passed, he just lay there, exhausted, wrapped up in Darric. Trying to pretend he could stay like that forever. Trying to pretend his life wasn't well and truly over. Trying, desperately trying, not to hate himself, because he was going to be on his own for a very long time.

"I think you needed that."

Darric's soft words teased Aden. *Darric*. He loved him so much. Another sob worked its way free, as his heart squeezed in anguish. The cage had hurt, but this was unbearable.

Darric let go of Aden. He felt the bed dip and heard Darric go to the bathroom. Aden turned on his side and tried to roll himself up into a ball. He was so tired, and his head was pounding. The bed moved and Darric gently rolled him over. He tugged at the towel, and Aden tried to grab it as Darric pulled it away.

"No, no." Panic threaded Aden's cracked voice. "You can't see me." *You can't ever see me.*

"Hush, beautiful boy. You didn't dry yourself properly. I don't want you getting sore."

Aden's breath hitched as a warm towel gently scraped his abdomen. *No, no further, please God.* But Darric was relentless and continued to pat his groin in smooth, soft motions, drying the damp hairs there gently. Aden nearly wept again when he felt Darric cup his balls. "Open your eyes. Look at me." *No, never.*

"Aden, open your eyes, beautiful boy."

The words wove around Aden, and he blinked, unable to hold against the seductive, compelling whispers.

"I think this is worse in your imagination than reality." Darric slid down the bed a little. "I think you are forgetting—" Darric softly breathed a kiss on Aden's belly, the barest whisper of lips on sensitive skin. "—how gorgeous you are to all your mates."

"No, I—"

"Hush." Darric breathed the word on his skin once more. "Just relax. Let me love you."

Aden sank a little deeper into the bed, his mind protesting, but his body relenting under Darric's spell. Darric's lips pressed into his skin. Aden blinked in awe, and closed his eyes. Darric...he was kissing his scars. Darric mouthed the ugly, red flesh with his soft lips and sinful words. Aden was being told, over and over, how he was loved, how he was precious, and as Darric's hot mouth closed over his cock, Aden nearly cried again; Darric didn't just make love to his body, Darric was caressing his mind. It felt like Darric held his very soul in the palm of that big, gentle hand.

He vaguely heard a door open. Suddenly, his nose was teased by the soft scent of lemons, as another hand cupped his cheek and pulled his head around. He nearly wept with delight when he saw Conner.

"I couldn't stay away any longer," Connor insisted.

Aden stared into Conner's eyes, and his breath hitched as he saw the unshed tears swimming in them. "Conner. I—" How could he tell him? How could Aden tell him how desperately he needed him—how much he needed all of them—but was so afraid?

Conner stripped off his clothes in seconds and as Darric settled once more to kissing him, Conner stole his mouth. Hot, wet kisses made his thoughts and fears spin away, until Conner broke free and latched onto Aden's neck.

Oh... he was marking him. *Yes.*

Aden thrust his hips, unable to keep still. "Darric. I—" Aden babbled incoherently as fire licked at his spine, screamed in frustration when the feeling didn't go any further. In complete desperation, Aden pushed futilely at the hard chest that imprisoned him, protected him, loved him. "Stop." Aden screamed, as he beat pointless fists on Darric's smooth skin. "Stop."

Aden sobbed in hysterical grief. No more, he couldn't take any more. "Please." His voice cracked, begging, pleading, unsure for what, and even the strong arms cradling his wrecked body gave him no comfort. Eventually, he lay still, exhausted, Conner and Darric both silent, just petting him gently in turn. He knew they were both trying to offer comfort, but it was pointless. He was right, they couldn't bond, he knew. "Aden, hush. Sleep." Conner dropped a kiss that Aden barely felt on his cheek.

Blaze. He wasn't here, he hadn't come back with Conner.

As soon as Conner was well, he would leave. Blaze hadn't returned, he obviously knew it was pointless, his Alpha's very absence told him more than words ever would.

Chapter Twelve

A DEN FELT LIKE HE had been awake a long time, just breathing slowly. He was trying to make sense in his own mind what had happened. Darric and Conner had made it perfectly clear how they felt, but...that was the problem. Even if by some miracle Aden could find a way, Blaze hadn't come back, and he would have known. *Where is he?* What if...what if Blaze was so disgusted he couldn't bear to even look at him? Conner stirred and Aden tried to calm his pounding heart. He wasn't really ready for an interrogation. He closed his eyes and willed himself to relax.

When Aden woke again, it was to clanking noises as two guys he had never seen before put trays down on the table in the corner of the room where Darric directed them. Heat bloomed in Aden's face and he quickly dragged the sheet up to cover Conner's naked body. Aden smiled at the protesting sound Conner made, and Darric closed the door behind the two men.

Aden's belly chose at that moment to churn loudly. Darric took a sip of coffee and walked nearer to him. He smiled and waved the cup at Aden. "Smell the coffee, baby." Aden smiled weakly and inhaled. He opened his mouth to beg for a sip, but his stomach dived as if he had just stepped on a rollercoaster. Aden snapped his mouth closed quickly.

Crap.

Aden scrambled for the bathroom, almost running into Darric. He just made it to the toilet before his stomach heaved up all its contents. Aden gasped and moaned, clutching the rim as he retched once more. He felt steadying hands on his head, and someone reached around with a cloth to wipe his mouth.

"Baby, Aden...what is it?" Conner rinsed the cloth and placed it on the back of his neck, cool this time. Aden couldn't answer, because he heaved once more. He heard soothing murmurs from Darric.

He panted miserably, laid his now pounding head back on Conner's chest, tried to breathe slowly through his nose. The nausea was passing a little.

"Water, sweetheart." Darric had brought a glass and handed it to Conner. Conner rested it at Aden's lips, and he took a cautious sip. It was cold, better.

Aden closed his eyes, and just breathed quietly.

"I think we need to get you off this floor." Darric bent down and lifted Aden. Aden murmured a little in protest at the movement but Darric cradled him like he was made of porcelain.

Conner lay down, opened his arms wide, and Darric placed Aden gently in them. "I'm going to find Blaze and the doctor."

"No, I'm okay," Aden protested. He wasn't sure about bothering Blaze, and doctors terrified him.

"Hush, sweetie. We just want to make sure you're well." Conner brushed a kiss on Aden's head. "Humor us, please."

Aden swallowed. He could feel a blush starting. "Stay?" He couldn't help the request, even though he knew he had to start doing things on his own.

"Of course I will. Aden, I understand about the doctor but Mike is a really nice guy. Do you remember Debbie? She helped take care of you before." Aden nodded. "Well, they're mates. Got three grown-up sons. One is away at medical school, and two are here, gammas."

Aden jumped when suddenly the door was slammed so wide it was a wonder it didn't come off its hinges. Blaze rushed in. "Aden, you're sick?" Aden cringed back against Conner at the noise, and Blaze halted at his reaction. "Aden..."

Aden felt awful. He'd just jumped at the noise, but now Blaze thought he was frightened of him. He started to speak, but Darric came in with the guy he had seen tending to Kellan's face.

"I'll leave you to it," Blaze said, and Aden swallowed. He wanted Blaze to stay, he just didn't know how to ask.

"Can I just press on your abdomen a little?" Aden blinked as the door closed behind Blaze. He turned his head nervously to the doctor.

"I—okay," Aden agreed, but he clasped Conner's hand tightly.

But it didn't hurt. The doctor prodded him gently, then seemed at a loss. "I can't find anything amiss. You are still undernourished though. Weres need a higher calorie content than humans, faster metabolism."

"But I don't shift," Aden blurted out.

The doctor shook his head. "Doesn't matter. You still have the healing properties of a shifter body that takes greater energy." He shook his head as he pulled down Aden's t-shirt over the myriad of scars that decorated his chest and abdomen. The doctor raised his eyebrows to Conner. "He needs to be kept well rested and well fed. Any further repeat of the vomiting, call me." Aden thanked the man, and Darric showed him out.

Conner nuzzled Aden's neck. "How about a nap?"

"No, it's the meeting, and I'm needed." Aden sat up cautiously; he really did feel much better. He grinned at Conner and Darric's identical frowns. "You heard the doctor, there's nothing wrong with me."

Aden slid out of bed and walked on perfectly steady legs to the table. He avoided the coffee pot, snagged a piece of bacon, and went to curl up in the big chair by the corner. As soon as he sat down he regretted it. The last time he had sat here had been on Blaze's knee. He suddenly couldn't stomach the bacon; his hand dropped away from his lips.

Darric gently took it from Aden's shaking fingers. "You have to eat, you will make yourself sick again."

"Where's Blaze? Doesn't he need to eat?" Conner asked.

Darric shook his head. "He ate earlier. I think he's more wound up over this morning than he wants us to believe."

Aden couldn't help giving Darric a worried look.

"Aden—" Darric started, only to be cut off as Ben entered the room.

"Alpha Blaze asked me to let you know the first delegation have cleared the far gates. They will be here in thirty minutes, sir." Conner nodded and thanked Ben as he left the room.

"Tell me again what will be happening today," Aden said, hoping to distract Darric from talking about food. He took a sip of his water, and rammed some bacon into his mouth. He nearly choked.

Conner sat back with a frustrated sigh. "I can manage today without you, Aden. You need to rest."

Aden glanced at Conner. He still looked as white as a sheet.

"I don't think so," Darric nearly growled.

Aden studied them both. "I'll be there. I know this is important." Conner needed him to cope with all the emotions that Aden knew would be present.

Conner put his cup down. "Blaze will be frantic," he said. "I know no one will be able to tell, but he's worked for years for this, for peace."

"Then we ought to go." Aden stood and went into the smaller room for some clothes. "Tell me again why everyone's decided to start meeting now."

Conner explained. "In the eighteenth and nineteenth centuries, werewolves were commonly accepted by humans. At the start of the First World War, our assistance was offered to the U.S. government, but it was turned down. For different reasons, the U.S. only got involved in the war officially in 1917. At that point the humans asked for help from the ruling werewolf council, but it was turned down as the werewolf packs were then fighting for dominance amongst themselves, and the ruling council fell apart. We struck a deal that the werewolves would be kept out of human conflict providing their existence remained relatively hidden."

Aden dressed, barely noticing what he put on as he waited for Conner to continue.

"Obviously the governments still knew, but the general public in the main did not," Darric continued. "The American government has now decided that werewolves represent a great weapon in the war on terrorism, and as such, now want to talk."

"And they want to talk to you?" Aden glanced at their solemn faces.

"The Jefferson pack Alpha, Hunter, has two nephews with government contacts," Darric said. "When we made ourselves and our intentions known to the Alpha, his two nephews arranged secret talks to get things moving.

This is still very unofficial, but it's a start."

"You know I don't doubt you for one second," Aden said slowly, "but how was the Jefferson Alpha convinced?"

"When we first appeared on Jefferson's lands, Blaze being Blaze marched straight up to the gates and demanded to see Hunter. His gammas took that as a challenge and immediately went to imprison him. Blaze bested five of them before one of them saw sense and called a halt to the whole thing."

Aden sighed a little. *More lives lost.*

"He didn't kill them, Aden. He could have easily, as you know, but he doesn't kill to prove a point."

Aden lifted his eyes to Conner. "Can you hear me?"

Conner shook his head sadly. "No, but I didn't need to, to see what you were thinking. You're very expressive."

"Anyway," continued Darric, "we were taken immediately to see Hunter. Hunter could tell how powerful Blaze was. We talked. Hunter has been a big help in his warnings about Senator Addison."

"Warnings?" Aden remembered the cruel woman and the awful lipstick.

Conner nodded. "She wants to introduce a draft, a military conscription service for all shifters, says it's the only way to control their 'baser' personalities." Sarcasm coated Conner's words.

"But surely, in this day and age, something like that would never happen."

Darric's face saddened. "People still fear what they don't understand, Aden. Centuries of teachings haven't, or are ever likely to change that basic human flaw. The Senator has the money to make people frightened. Blaze needs this meeting to be a success. The Senator wants the exact opposite." Aden leaned back, saddened.

Conner smiled and touched his face gently. Aden leaned into the contact. Conner touched him the most of them all, and Aden thought he needed the reassurance as much as he himself did.

Darric stood up. "I'm going to make sure everything's okay with Blaze while you two sleepy heads finish getting ready." He stroked a finger down Conner's cheek. "Are you strong enough?" He glanced at Aden. "We can probably manage today without either of you."

Conner shook his head. "You need me to read their emotions." He turned to Aden. "And I need you."

Aden nodded. He knew they both needed him, he was just very much afraid that Blaze never would.

Aden stood in the corner of the room while he waited for Conner, gazing out the window. The huge bedroom was in one corner of the house and his favorite part was the wrap around view from this window, perched right on the end of the house—meaning he could see in nearly all directions. The workers downstairs had completed the building that Aden had seen them erecting when he'd walked around the property. He couldn't believe that was almost two weeks ago.

Conner came out of the bathroom, and Aden nodded in approval. He was wearing his usual jeans with a soft bronze color polo shirt that matched his eyes.

Conner grinned. "I didn't know you were such an authority on clothing, but I'm glad you approve." Conner caught Aden's lips teasingly. "I'm an authority on clothing myself. *How to take it off.*"

Aden moved his head away as Conner's lips sought his—he couldn't, he had to focus, and thinking about how Conner's jeans were molded to his ass wasn't helping him do that. Fortunately, the door opened and Aden caught the scent of the outdoors.

"Everyone's here," Darric said solemnly. Aden moved away from Conner. They all left the room and walked steadily towards the meeting room where they had seen the Senator a few days ago.

Conner and Darric suddenly came to an abrupt halt and shot each other a horrified glance. Aden looked startled at them both, especially when he felt the distress building up in Connor.

"What is it?" Aden looked frantically at the pair of them. He had a bad feeling about this.

Darric pulled Aden to the side of the empty corridor. "Blaze doesn't want you and Conner at the meeting." Conner looked furious and nodded at Aden.

"Why, what's wrong? What's happened?"

"Senator Addison?" Darric said. "She's here with a new advisor." Conner moved to hold Aden close. Darric looked wretched. "It's...your old pack doctor."

Sick dread bolted Aden's feet to the floor. "But I thought they were all dead."

Darric shook his head. "The Alpha and the gammas, certainly. The old beta as well, but the doctor disappeared and Blaze was desperate to get you to me so we could start the healing. Blaze won't put you or Conner through this."

Aden agreed, the thought of looking at that evil man terrified him. He was quite happy to leave it to Blaze. Aden turned to walk back, and then stopped at Conner's awed voice.

"How is it that Blaze hasn't killed the man already?"

He thought about how many times Blaze had come to his rescue, about how gentle he had been with him. How the current impossible situation was all his own stupid fault, and how desperately and without thanks Blaze was trying to protect not just his own family, but ultimately all humanity. It was humbling. The man had given so much of himself, and all Aden had to do was walk into a room.

"No." Aden planted his feet.

Darric's eyebrows rose questioningly, but Conner chuckled. "Quite right, little omega."

Darric glanced, seeming puzzled, at Conner.

"Darric." Aden pulled at his arm. "Blaze needs Conner, and if it's right what you say, you all need me."

Conner nodded. "You're not telling me you don't think this is too much of a coincidence, Darric. This has been done deliberately hoping to throw us off."

Darric smiled slowly. "You're both right, I can smell the deceit from here."

Aden smirked. "That's not deceit. The doctor was never fond of spending a long time on personal hygiene."

Conner grinned and put his head to one side in thought. He blinked and looked at Aden. "Blaze doesn't like it, but says it's up to us. He also asks if you will agree to us being able to hear each other. He thinks it may be important for the meeting."

Aden sighed. He didn't want them to know his thoughts, especially Blaze. "Okay, tell him I agree. For the meeting only." He chose not to acknowledge the hurt that bloomed in Conner's eyes. He couldn't.

"He agrees and says you are to sit between him and Conner," Darric said. "Apparently I am promised my turn later."

Aden flushed, and tried not to let his mind go there. They had a job to do. He looked at Darric. "If the doctor is there, all the more reason for us to be there too."

Conner nodded. "Blaze thought someone in the pack knew of your importance. I think we just found out who."

Chapter Thirteen

Aden enjoyed every second of the astonishment on the Senator's face when he walked into the room. Her blood red lips, with the same god-awful lipstick painted on, gaped unattractively. He wasn't sure he had the courage to look at Gregory, so he just calmly walked towards Blaze's outstretched arm.

I need you next to me. Blaze looked apologetic at invading Aden's mind.

For now, Aden's traitorous heart echoed, *you want me for now,* and he was glad at least when Blaze didn't respond.

"I really don't think it's appropriate for your boyfriend to be present." The Senator's sarcastic drawl brought the room to a hushed silence. Aden was battered by emotions. Anger from Conner, but embarrassment from the row of guys who sat in suits in the front row facing them around the table. He didn't even glance at the doctor—the satisfaction was pouring off him in waves.

It was Darric who spoke up. "My apologies, gentleman, and Senator Addison. We have not introduced the fourth member of our ruling circle, and I can understand his youthfulness may be confusing to um...more mature individuals."

Aden nearly snorted and Senator Addison practically ground her teeth. Darric had just very politely called the woman old.

"But please don't take that as an indication of ability. Aden is likely the most powerful omega to have ever lived. Our ability to help the government hinges on his ability to help us."

Aden gripped Blaze's hand tightly as everyone's heads swung in his direction. He tried to look serene and willed himself not to blush. And to look, well...*old*. It wasn't helping that he could nearly hear the amusement pouring off Conner.

One of the rather stern looking men in the front row spoke up. "Perhaps you could enlighten those of us not familiar with werewolf politics what an omega is. I understand from your indication of importance it must differ somewhat from the Greek definition."

Darric smiled and Aden could see the man relax a little.

"An omega is responsible for the emotional well-being of the pack."

"Like a counselor?" put in another guy who looked interested.

"Like a shrink," added another derisively. Aden looked up at that remark. The guy who'd made it sat on the other side of the Senator.

"Aden has no medical training whatsoever," the doctor put in smoothly.

Darric still smiled, ignored the comments, and pulled the discussion back around to exactly what the government was wanting. One of the guys in uniform who sat immediately in front of Blaze took charge of his side, blatantly ignoring the Senator whenever she tried unsuccessfully to interrupt.

She's not making friends, Aden thought, and surreptitiously gazed at the Senator who was starting to look very foolish indeed. Aden refocused on Darric again.

Blaze and Darric were an incredible team. Every time Blaze stipulated something, Darric elaborated until he had people agreeing. Darric listed the clear benefits of werewolves in warfare, ranging from superior strength and speed to having superior scent abilities to assist with the location of IED's, which made quite a few of the guys that were in military uniform sit up and take notice. His low, melodic voice was practically pulling the humans into his way of thinking.

Blaze then clearly laid out the conditions training would have to include. Full moon runs were explained in great detail to the fascination of most of the guys assembled. He also explained pack membership and loyalties, at which point one of the guys in a uniform interrupted.

"Alpha?" Aden was pleased to see Blaze being addressed respectfully. "I foresee two initial problems, if I may." Blaze nodded. "Firstly, the most obvious one being not all humans are aware of werewolves, and the implications of that are quite staggering. We have no idea of how our NATO allies will react, and as such we would like you to consider separately trained groups rather than a general assimilation."

Aden saw a lot of nods around the room at that statement. He felt the satisfaction rolling off Blaze and Darric.

Connor nudged Aden surreptitiously. *That was exactly what we were hoping for.*

"Secondly." Aden saw the human stare at Darric and relax slightly. "We are worried the chain of command may be a huge issue. We understand pack loyalties, but what would happen if a werewolf was given a direct order by a human that countermanded an order by his Alpha?"

Blaze spoke. "I understand, and I appreciate that is a valid concern. I think that is why making separate units may be the answer." Blaze paused, and Aden knew something big was coming. "However I don't think the units should be werewolf only." Several uniformed guys sat up straighter. "I think it is vital that the units are split between experienced human soldiers and werewolf recruits. They may have superior physical abilities to utilize, but they have no experience in the sort of combat and weapons usage you will be requiring."

"You're almost talking up a buddy system here," one of the other officers interrupted.

Blaze's eyes swung to him. "Exactly."

Darric leaned forward to the same man. Aden nearly grinned at the reaction—the poor guy put an uncomfortable finger around his collar. Darric looked surprised and leaned back immediately.

The guy in charge glanced around at his colleagues. "From our point of view, we would be very interested in discussing that idea." Agreed murmurs rose, and Aden felt the warning from Conner flash around a second before Senator Addison opened her mouth.

"No one is mentioning the real danger to our men should these savages become uncontrollable."

Most of the other humans gasped or paled at the insult, but a few of them who sat near the Senator nodded in agreement. Aden leaned around Blaze and touched Darric. He already had a hand on Conner. One of the "suits" that had been listening intently while the military personnel spoke interrupted immediately.

"Senator Addison, might I remind you that you are here by virtue of a very recent appointment? You have neither the experience nor clearly the discipline required to be involved in these sorts of negotiations. If you cannot keep your damn fool mouth shut, I will have one of my men escort you from the building, and I don't give a rat's ass who your daddy is."

Aden felt the shared delight bounce around the room, and smiled surreptitiously to himself.

The man suddenly turned to Aden. "We haven't met, but if you're part of their support team, I guess we should." He stood and offered his hand to Aden. "I'm Senator Bud Mason."

Aden stood politely. "Aden Laney." He shook hands with the Senator, his blue eyes twinkling under the shockingly huge salt and pepper eyebrows. Aden grinned, he liked the man already. He sat down and rested his hand discreetly on Conner's leg, under the table, and felt the contentment pouring off him.

Blaze lifted lazy eyes at the Senator. Aden looked hard at Blaze; he was surprised he hadn't ripped the woman's head off.

Conner nudged Aden's hand. *A month ago he would have. Our combined tempers would have made it impossible to deal with such ignorance and prejudice.*

But now, he only has to worry about himself. He's mad, don't get me wrong, but he's controlling the anger.

Aden kept a tight hold of Conner and felt a little pride for the first time in his life.

Blaze suddenly stood up, and Aden felt the spark of fear in at least ten people in the room.

The Senator continued babbling. "Of course, I have been working with Dr. Madden here." Aden breathed out slowly. He wasn't going to be much use to Blaze if he let his own emotions get the better of him. He'd already caught the subtle stiffening of Conner. "Dr. Madden, a werewolf himself, has done extensive research into assisting werewolves in controlling their *baser* personalities."

Aden could see Blaze forcibly keep himself in check, although from Blaze's polite mask, not one person in the room would have been able to tell.

Aden noted again how the group surrounding the Senator were murmuring agreement. The humans might not want to appear rude, but they obviously shared similar fears. One of the other men in uniform interrupted then. "Sir?" Most people turned as the guy stood awkwardly. He was wearing a uniform so Aden assumed him to be military, but as he stood awkwardly and rested his hip, Aden suddenly realized from the way his pants hung he was struggling with an artificial leg.

Blaze looked at the guy respectfully.

"Surely the initial problems wouldn't be in the field," the man said. "The first and most practical problems would be training. I imagine a team should look initially at converting one of our smaller bases perhaps? I can think of one or two that have direct access to woodland areas suitable for the runs, especially as this will need to be secret for some considerable time."

Blaze stood and walked over to the man extending his hand. "I think that's an excellent idea..." Blaze paused with his hand extended.

"Marcus Flint." The two guys shook hands. Aden was surprised; he'd expected the man to introduce himself with a rank, but then he didn't know anything about soldiers. Aden glanced down to the guy's leg as he shifted his weight again.

Maybe he didn't have a rank because of his injury, surely he wouldn't be able to fight anymore.

Blaze looked at Senator Mason. "I think we can make serious progress here."

Senator Addison made a disapproving noise.

Senator Mason completely ignored Senator Addison again. He stood up and met Blaze with an outstretched hand. "I think we just outstayed our welcome for today. Alpha, you have been most generous with your time and information. I know a few of our military personnel are very excited at the prospect of collaboration." He gestured to the guys in uniforms who had also stood, and was met with affirmative nods. "Perhaps a smaller group would be beneficial to work out details before we can present it to my superiors?"

Darric drew the guy to one side while he and Blaze talked. Aden noted with satisfaction how Marcus looked to be included. Senator Addison postured and went to join in, but was smoothly deflected by two of Senator Mason's staff. Conner leaned back; Aden turned, concerned. Conner looked tired, but at least everybody was leaving.

One of the gammas came up and spoke briefly to Conner. Aden was incredibly pleased with how things had gone.

"So, you seem to have done well for yourself."

The voice of Gregory Madden slid over his skin, and Aden just managed to stop the full body shiver that the man's smooth words caused him. He was astonished that the doctor had the guts to approach him when the walls were flanked by Blaze's gammas, to say nothing of the man himself. Aden looked back at the doctor and stood a little taller.

"It wasn't personal, you know," Madden pressed.

Aden felt the wave of anger behind him, and turned to see Conner. He counted to five before he opened his mouth. He wanted to make sure his voice was steady. "*Personal?* It was very personal." Aden watched the doctor shuffle his feet slightly. "You encouraged both Alphas to beat and torture me for nearly a year. My parents were slaughtered and you did nothing to help them, or to help me." Aden felt Conner at his back. "How could you encourage him? You're supposed to be a doctor."

Madden glanced behind Aden and paled slightly. Aden knew from the faint scent that Darric now stood behind him too.

"He was insane. He'd threatened my family for years." The doctor stammered, clearly intimidated. His voice took on a faintly whining tone.

Aden shook his head in disbelief. He remembered when the doctor had been present during his beatings. He'd not objected once. It never looked like he was under any duress—he looked to be enjoying it.

The doctor looked over Aden's shoulder and took a step back. Aden knew that meant Blaze had now arrived, and the doctor gulped at Blaze's low growl.

"It was only out of respect for the Senator and my wish not to disrupt the meeting that you were allowed on our lands at all. But know this: you will never have access to any pack. From this day you aren't welcome anywhere that recognizes our Alpha triad, nor Orion's Circle."

"Alpha. Alpha, please—" Gregory started protesting and taking more steps backward, but he stopped when he backed into Blaze's gamma.

"I suggest you leave, before my generosity is stretched further." Blaze nodded to the retreating group with Senator Addison. "If I ever see you again on our property, you will be put down." Blaze turned to Aden, and spoke formally. "Omega, do you require any further reparation for your parents' deaths?"

Aden looked at the man. He'd terrified him for so long, but now he was whining pathetically. Most bullies after all were cowards at heart. Aden should be gratified, but he just felt sick. "I don't think he should practice medicine anywhere." Healing was a euphemism that shouldn't be applied to this evil man.

"Agreed." Blaze nodded to two of his gammas and the doctor was hastened from the room.

Aden sighed and leaned back into Blaze's warmth. "Is he going to cause trouble for you?"

"I'd like to see him try," Darric bit off a furious response.

Aden suddenly realized what he was doing, and his heart beat a little faster. Blaze was slowly rubbing his hands up and down Aden's arms. Then, as Blaze also seemed to become aware, he stepped away. "Senator Mason apologized for their presence. He doesn't know who the doctor is, but he was shanghaied with Senator Addison being here.

Aden stood quietly and watched as the last of the gammas left with the visitors.

"She shouldn't have been present at all."

Aden turned at the new voice. Three guys had walked in. Aden could smell they were shifters straight away. He backed up a little, suspiciously, until he hit Conner's reassuring chest. They must have been friends though, because Blaze and Darric immediately greeted them with expressions of pleasure.

Conner wrapped his arms around Aden. "Aden, this is Hunter, Alpha of Jefferson pack."

All three guys suddenly turned their attention to Aden. Aden was amazed at how good looking they were. He didn't remember his own pack having such attractive guys. He smiled appreciatively.

Conner growled softly, and Hunter raised his eyebrows questioningly. One of the guys next to the Alpha put out his hand. "Omega, my name is Michael. I am honored to meet you. Please let me know if Jefferson can be of any service to you."

Aden nodded and then shook hands with all of them as they were introduced. The other guy was called Ricoh. Ricoh and Michael were both betas.

Blaze invited the three shifters to eat with them and they trooped to the dining room. Aden studied them all while Blaze and Darric updated them on the meeting. Alpha Hunter looked older than Aden's three Alphas, but not by much. Shifters lived long lives, but he wouldn't have put him over forty, the other two maybe in their late twenties. Hunter was talking to Blaze and he was struck by the similarity in their dark coloring. Ricoh seemed the quietest of the three. He kept his fair head bent throughout most of the meal.

"We noticed the doctor from Black Lakes pack leaving. We also saw him get in the car with the Senator."

Aden heard the respectful tone that Hunter used, but understood the question behind it.

Blake sighed. "We had no idea he would be there. Senator Mason I have the deepest respect for, but I suspect his hands are tied by finances."

"What do you mean?" Aden asked curiously.

"The introduction of weres in the military wouldn't come cheap. Specialized body armor, for one."

"How on earth could wolves wear body armor?" Aden's head was spinning. "I mean, if they shifted it would be lost…"

"And no workable thumbs after they shift?" Connor added teasingly. Blaze nodded. "Exactly where the human partner would come in." Aden sat back, stunned. The whole thing was remarkably clever. "We've had a lot of time to plan this, little one."

Aden glanced at Blaze. Those deep blue eyes were regarding him steadily. He was so confused.

"So, if I may, Alphas." Michael leaned forward. "The idea is that a small group will be set up to investigate the proper use of wolves in the military? But with the intention, as far as is possible, to try and keep this out of the public domain?"

Blaze nodded. "But only until we get established. Once this is operational, it will be impossible, but by then it will be a fait accompli. You know, you would have been welcome to attend the meeting."

"We actually came to tell you something else, Alpha." Hunter glanced at Aden.

Aden sat up. He could feel concern and didn't need to see Hunter's face to know it was something to do with him.

Conner growled low. Aden touched him automatically, and Conner visibly relaxed.

"That's incredible." Everyone turned in surprise at the softly spoken words. It was Ricoh. He flushed bright red and dipped his head. "My apologies, Alphas."

Darric reached out reassuringly. "No need."

Aden caught the benevolent glance Hunter sent Ricoh, and immediately wondered at their relationship.

"This is to do with Black Lakes pack, what there is left of it anyway. Kellan has been very helpful in giving us background into the pack," Hunter said.

Aden stiffened automatically at hearing Kellan's name, but he listened carefully.

"Apparently around two hundred years ago, the pack lost the ability to heal wounds by shifting," Hunter continued. Aden glanced at Darric as Darric gasped, and remembered he hadn't been there when they were talking about it. Aden thought all packs were the same, and healing injuries had been something of legends only.

Blaze glanced at Darric. "We knew something was wrong, but we hadn't realized how far back it went."

"We could be wrong." Hunter paused and glanced uncomfortably at Aden. "But we think the doctor and the old Black Lakes Alpha have been experimenting with genetics. With Kellan's and a few of the younger gammas' help, we've uncovered what looks to be a lab. The worrying thing is, we think the old Alpha was actually approaching three hundred, not the hundred he was supposed to be, and his genetic experiments were poisoning the pack's true lines, which is why they'd lost the healing ability."

"This was why the doctor encouraged him to keep the omega." Hunter smiled at Aden. "His experiments with immortality were warping his mind. It was only the cruelty he displayed that kept him half sane, if you can use that word. We believe the doctor knew this."

Blaze nodded to two of the gammas that were by the door. "I want Doctor Madden found and detained. As soon as he is caught, bring him to me." The two shifters disappeared silently.

"Alpha?" Aden cleared his throat and addressed Hunter nervously. "How—" He swallowed nervously.

"Aden has good friends among Black Lakes," Blaze put in smoothly. "He is particularly anxious to get news of Jay. Kellan's younger brother, actually."

"Jay?" Hunter repeated, and smiled at Aden's nod. "I will find out. How old is Jay?"

"Eighteen. Same age as me." Aden blushed a little under the Alpha's firm gaze.

Michael interrupted. "Then he will be fine. All the younger weres are being kept with their family groups."

Aden nodded, pleased. Everyone stood, and Hunter, Michael, and Ricoh left. They all turned to troop back upstairs. Aden knew Conner was exhausted and Aden fixed a look on Blaze, hesitating. There was so much he wanted to say. *Blaze?*

Blaze didn't even glance at him, and Aden's heart thumped. He'd asked him to turn his thoughts off and Blaze obviously had. He'd got what he wanted...so, why did that hurt so much?

Chapter Fourteen

Conner was dragging his feet by the time they reached their room, and Blaze turned and clucked at him, concerned. "It was too much for you today. I should have insisted you both stayed here and rested, or better yet shift and go for a run. You made the negotiations much easier," Blaze said, turning to smile at Aden to include him in the comment, but Aden glanced away and pretended he hadn't seen.

He caught the worried look Darric threw Blaze, but Aden was too miserable to care. Aden and Darric walked with Connor and helped him sit on the bed. Conner smiled up at him.

"You must be tired," Aden said, and he yanked off his shoes and shirt but left his pants where they were. Conner shrugged out of his clothes, and Blaze bent down and undid his shoes. Aden paused then, something suddenly occurring to him. "Conner, why can't you just shift now? And why didn't you just shift—" Aden flushed. It was his fault Conner had been sick.

Conner smiled. "Shifting only heals physical injuries or ailments, Aden, and I would rather wait and run tomorrow. It's the full moon."

Aden nodded and lay down, drawing Conner into him. He'd completely forgotten about the moon. Aden dropped a kiss on Conner's head. "How about we both take a nap?"

Darric toed off his sneakers and his clothes followed too. Aden deliberately didn't look.

"Blaze?" Conner smiled and stretched his hand out. Aden held his breath. Blaze caught Conner's hand and drew it to his mouth.

"I'm going to grab a quick shower then check if the gammas have detained Madden," Blaze said. Aden stilled at the exquisite sight of the huge man dropping a gentle kiss on the hand he held. He blinked furiously.

"Blaze, you haven't had any proper sleep in over a week," Darric chided gently.

Blaze glanced at Aden as he straightened. The sorrowful look headed straight for Aden's heart. "I will, later." Blaze dropped his glance and headed for the bathroom. Aden stared at the door that Blaze closed quietly.

"He can't sleep because he feels responsible for your injuries," Connor put in quietly.

Aden frowned. "But that's ridiculous. How could it possibly be his fault?" After all, it was Aden's stupidity that had brought them here.

"I agree," Conner put in. "I mean, if we're going to assign blame, it was really my fault."

Aden pulled Conner towards him protectively. "How on earth—"

Conner shrugged. "If I hadn't been so sick, Blaze would have come and checked on you sooner."

"But that wasn't your fault. You're an empath. It's what you are," Aden protested.

"Actually it was my fault," said Darric quietly. "If I had Conner's talent, I would have known far earlier that something was wrong."

Aden was getting quite worked up now. He sat up. "Darric, you are one of the most selfless people I know." He looked at Conner. "You both are. How can you possibly blame yourselves for something some maniac did?"

Darric put a hand out and stroked Aden's face. "Exactly, omega, how could we?"

Aden opened his mouth to continue his tirade, then snapped it shut as Darric's words registered. Aden's shoulders slumped a little and he gave a sheepish smile.

"There is someone else that needs to learn that lesson." Darric nodded to the bathroom door, then calmly ignored Aden and drew a sleepy Conner into his embrace.

Aden stared at them. Conner had his eyes closed and Darric was pressing kisses down his neck. Aden brought his hand around to his front. The sight of them never failed to arouse him. He stilled as that thought registered and he started to harden. Harden? He'd thought himself permanently damaged, but he realized feeling was returning to his groin. His shifter body was healing and his heart was pounding so hard, it felt like it was going to escape his chest. He concentrated and knew Blaze had turned his thoughts off. The only last thing was his fear that Blaze couldn't get past his scars. He didn't want him out of pity. Then Aden shook his head as he realized how he had just insulted his Alpha. Blaze wasn't so shallow. It wasn't Blaze who was struggling to get past his scars, it was Aden.

He heard a soft sound from the bed and his own lips curved at the knowing smile from Darric. Conner was fast asleep and cushioned protectively on Darric's shoulder. He wanted that. He wanted to belong to them more than he wanted his heart to beat. Aden's smile deepened. Darric closed his eyes, looking incredibly content. Aden got off the bed and headed for the bathroom.

The sound of the water deadened the noise of the door and Aden entered quietly and watched Blaze. The man stood in the shower, head bowed, dejection visible in the defeated slump of his shoulders, unmoving as the water pounded onto his back. Aden must have made some noise, some sound, because the second he decided his Alpha needed him, Blaze lifted his head and pierced his gaze.

Aden stared, shocked. The stark lines of defeat were in every line around Blaze's mouth and every shadow in his eyes.

"Blaze, open your mind. *Please.*"

Blaze blinked. He hesitated. "Are you sure?"

"I've never been so sure of anything in my whole life." Aden let his pants drop, keeping his eyes firmly on Blaze.

Do you want me? Me? Not because I'm an omega, but because I'm Aden?

Blaze reached out an arm and pulled Aden into the shower with him. A large hand cupped his face. "I want you more than my next breath." Aden stared as his Alpha drew his smaller hand to his lips. "My darling, it kills me that I was unable to prevent any harm coming to you."

Aden pressed his fingers onto Blaze's lips to hush him. "I was stupid—"

"You were loyal. This wasn't your fault."

"Blaze, it wasn't yours either." He looked down at his shorts, which were completely soaked by the shower, his thickening erection very visible.

Blaze stiffened and drew back. "It doesn't matter. It would never have mattered. Don't come in here because you think I only want you because of that." Blaze's voice broke. He was visibly shaken, his head lowered. Aden placed the palm of his hand on the man's rough cheek.

"Blaze, Blaze. Look at me." Aden drew Blaze's head up with his hand. "You have to see it from my side. I spent years being a failure." Blaze opened his mouth, but Aden shook his head to silence him. "It seemed I failed at everything, *everything.*" Aden's hand nearly shook with intensity. It was so important Blaze understood. "Then these three amazing powerful guys told me I was their mate." Aden smiled into the intense blue eyes staring at him. "I mean, three?" Aden smirked a little. "Don't forget, old man, you've had six hundred years to get used to that idea."

Blaze laughed and pulled Aden close. Aden grimaced. "If you can stand to see my scars, I could really do to get out of these shorts."

Blaze bent his head while his fingers pulled at the elastic and peeled them away.

"What do you think?" Blaze's hand lazily traced its way from the lips it was brushing to under Aden's chin, and headed lower, grazing Aden's chest and abdomen. By the time he'd reached his belly, Aden's knees were seriously in danger of giving way. Blaze bent his head and murmured in Aden's neck, as his fingers found the first scar and followed it. "I love your body, Aden. It belongs to me. It's perfect." Blaze's finger reached the tip of Aden's cock, and gently pushed in the slit. "How's it feel?"

Aden would have told him if he could have concentrated enough to actually do anything other than moan.

"Mmm," Blaze murmured as one of his large hands swept over Aden's chest. Teasing fingers found his nipple, and Aden was shot with such lust, his legs did give way, and Blaze caught him. Blaze spread his legs apart and leaned Aden further back into him. Blaze's cock was scraping his buttocks deliciously, and his own was rock hard.

"Let me take the edge off," Blaze murmured. He reached a soapy hand around to Aden's aching cock.

Aden twisted around, planting his feet. "No." Blaze looked after everyone. It was about time someone did a little something for him. Blaze's wonder hit his mind at the same time as Aden thought of it, and Aden slid to his knees. He looked at Blaze's huge cock, and grinned. It was perfectly in proportion to the rest of him really. Blaze's hands rested gently on the back of his head, and Aden brought his hands up, desperately wanting to taste him. He'd never actually done this before, and he wasn't sure how far he could go. He heard a low throated growl from Blaze, and knew his thoughts were turning him on. He hesitantly opened his mouth, and wound his fingers around the base.

You-you don't...have to do this.

Aden closed his mouth around Blaze's cock, heard the man's head bang back against the tiles. He groaned with desire. It was perfect, *he* was perfect. Aden was equally as turned on by the heady feeling of making Blaze lose a tiny bit of control, as he was by the taste of him. Perfect, he tongued his glans gently and he heard a throaty growl. *So sensitive.* Aden used his imagination, and listened very intently. He felt he could hear every gasp, every moan and every thud of Blaze's heart through the noise of the spray beating down on his back. Aden teased with his tongue and hollowed his cheeks as he sucked back. He could feel Blaze wobble and nearly crowed in delight. Aden bent and intensified his movements,

He swirled around the head with his tongue and gently scraped back with his teeth. He kissed and licked the man's tightly drawn up balls, but just couldn't open his mouth wide enough to get one inside. He pushed the top of his tongue onto Blaze's slit, and reveled in the gasp this caused.

"Aden," Blaze ground out. "I can't hold back if you keep doing that."

Aden would have rather died than stop. He backed his mouth up a little but kept tight hold, suddenly nervous. He hollowed his cheeks as he drew up slowly and with a harsh cry, Blaze stiffened and his cock pulsed. Aden started swallowing quickly, desperate not to let any of Blaze's cream escape. After several fierce bursts, Blaze hissed and pressed softly on Aden's head, a signal to slow down. He swallowed finally and gently smoothed his tongue around the head to make sure it was clean. Blaze lifted around his waist with firm hands and hoisted him up suddenly, his mouth still wide open from Blaze's cock, which had dropped from his lips.

With a groan, Blaze fastened his lips on Aden. Aden nearly dissolved in need as he realized Blaze could taste himself on Aden's lips. It was so hot; Aden was suddenly very aware of his own aching erection again. Blaze hoisted him up higher, and Aden wrapped his legs around Blaze's waist. Hungry, desperate kisses rained on every available part of his mouth and lips. Aden let his head fall back and Blaze fell on his throat. The burning under Blaze's mouth as he realized he was being marked, and the hot, wet friction of his cock against Blaze's stomach lit up Aden's body. He cried out as his balls pumped all over Blaze's chest. Gasping, shaking, he collapsed forward onto Blaze. He couldn't think, he didn't want to think.

Blaze bent his head and rested it so it was just touching Aden's. "Forgive me?"

Aden pushed into another kiss. He ran his tongue around the seam of Blaze's lips and bit down on the lower one. "I would if there was anything to forgive."

Blaze looked up, distress swimming in those blue eyes. "I was nearly too late. I don't know how you don't hate me."

"Blaze." Aden drew the man's big head down into his embrace. "How could I hate you when I love you so very much?"

Blaze stiffened, and for one awful moment Aden thought he'd said the wrong thing. His Alpha's head rose, the eyes round. "You love me?"

Aden nodded, suddenly feeling choked. He hoped he didn't have to say anything else. Blaze drew a gentle hand along Aden's forehead and smoothed the hair from his eyes. "Aden, I loved you from the moment I saw you in the clearing. You're mine, *mine*." Fierce, possessive, *wonderful*.

"Y-yes, yours." Blaze met Aden's mouth like a man possessed.

Suddenly the water was shut off. Aden opened his eyes as Darric draped warm towels around them both. Blaze made a desperate sound in the back of his throat and lifted Aden up to his body, as if he were frightened he was going to be taken away. Aden closed his eyes as satisfaction bathed him and Blaze, and they were guided back to bed. Guided because neither of them opened their eyes or stopped kissing the whole way.

Finally, Aden was pulled away from Blaze's wonderful lips. He whined in protest.

"My turn, beautiful."

Aden cracked his eyes open as the gray ones sparked with desire. He loved putting that light in them. Darric mouthed his lips softly, then laid Aden on the bed.

Chapter Fifteen

Aden sat exhausted on the bathroom floor when he heard the door open. "Baby, why didn't you wake me?" Blaze tried to scoop him up, but Aden turned his face away.

"Teeth." He pointed to the sink. Blaze nodded and steadied him while he brushed them, then stood patiently while he spat all the nastiness out of his mouth. He'd felt sick the second he'd opened his eyes this morning, and only just made it to the bathroom in time. He slumped back against Blaze, and Blaze lifted and cradled him to his chest.

"I'm going to get the doctor to see you again, this is ridiculous," Blaze said.

Aden didn't have the energy to care. He felt the kiss on his forehead as he was lowered into Conner's waiting arms. Barely heard the murmuring voices, as he drifted into sleep.

"Aden, wake up, sweetheart." Aden blinked. Darric's worried face looked down. He stood next to Debbie's mate, the doctor.

"Young man, I just need to take some blood samples, to see what's going on." Aden didn't get a chance to reply as the doctor efficiently had his arm extended and blood drawn before he had a chance to even think of a reply. He personally thought it was a lot of fuss about nothing. Worse things had happened to him than being sick a few times.

Sometime later, he could hear low murmurs from the corner by the bay window. He blinked sleepily. Darric and Blaze were huddled together over by the sofa. He sat up. "What is it?" Aden glanced over at Conner's supine form next to him, still fast asleep.

Blaze stood up, looking worried. "How are you feeling?

He got up and padded over to the table, trying really hard not to wince a little as he moved. He reached for coffee, then changed his mind and got some juice instead. Aden sipped, head down, still waiting patiently for one of them to answer. *You're not supposed to answer a question with a question.*

"There's nothing to worry about," Blaze put in hurriedly as Darric caught Aden and pulled him down next to him on the sofa instead.

Aden looked at Blaze. "People generally feel they need to say that for reassurance, usually when there is something to worry about." Aden took another sip. "Besides which I could sense it in both of you when I woke." Darric grinned and looked sheepishly at Blaze. "He's got us both there."

Blaze rubbed his face and Aden was struck by how tired he looked. "Did you get any rest?"

Darric shook his head, interrupting whatever Blaze was going to say.

"No, he hasn't. He hasn't had any proper sleep in days."

Blaze smiled. "You sound like your mother."

Darric slapped his forehead in mock horror. "In that case, you can gut the fish for the whole week." Aden watched, fascinated, as they both shared an amused look. He would have loved to have known them as little boys.

He put his glass down, and hesitantly stood. Blaze was hurting, and Aden was here drinking juice and doing nothing to help. "Blaze, please?"

In seconds, Blaze had opened his arms and seemed to pluck Aden from where he was standing. Aden rained kisses on his gorgeous man. "Why don't you shift and go for a run?"

Blaze nuzzled into his neck. "I will tonight. I'd rather stay here."

Darric snorted. "What he means is, he's not going to let you out of his sight for a minute."

Aden stood. "Come and lie with me then. Darric will get us when we are needed."

Blaze sighed and buried his head in Aden's chest. "I don't deserve you."

Aden smiled and poked him again. "Well, you're stuck with me. Deal with it." He stood and pulled Blaze's arm for him to follow. "Just for a little while," he pleaded.

Aden lay down and held his arm out towards Blaze, breathlessly. Would Blaze cuddle into him, or would he see it as a sign of weakness? Blaze never hesitated. He yawned. "Just for a little while then." He rested his head in the crook of Aden's arm. Aden thrilled at the weight of Blaze against him, and kissed the big man.

"I promise." Aden tightened his arms around his Alpha. Aden breathed quietly and listened to Blaze fall asleep. He dropped a kiss on Blaze's black hair just because he could. He closed his eyes and dozed a little, smiling when he felt a hand stroke the side of his face.

He opened his eyes into Conner's brown ones. Conner nodded towards Blaze, and whispered, "Good to see."

Aden smiled and turned his face to kiss the palm that was near it. Darric entered the room, and looked apologetic as Blaze blinked sleepily. Aden tutted. "You needed more." He doubted if he'd been asleep an hour.

He was met with a wide smile. "I need more of you." He glanced at Darric and reached over to touch Conner. "I need more of all of you."

Conner blew a kiss at him happily and Blaze lifted his head. "What time is it?"

"A little after nine. There's no rush."

"Do you have meetings today?" Aden asked.

Darric shook his head. "No, but you need rest today, you will have a busy night."

Aden blushed, and Conner snickered. "We don't mean that sort of busy." Then Conner grinned. "Well actually, we kind of do."

Blaze sat up, pulling Aden with him. "It's the full moon tonight."

Aden took a slow breath. Yes, yes it was. He could feel a little excitement run through his veins.

"And it's our bonding ceremony." Darric wiggled his eyebrows evilly at Aden.

Oh. "What—" He cleared his throat. "What does that mean?" Aden blushed. "I mean, I know what it means…" Aden stammered, only to be dragged back down by Connor, who fastened his lips to him in a punishing kiss. Finally, Connor broke away and pressed his forehead to him.

"You are so adorable when you blush."

Aden wriggled, happy to be adorable if that meant the chance of another kiss. Conner chuckled.

"Actually." Darric dragged Aden away from Connor, who immediately pouted until Blaze pulled him in for a kiss. "I'm not sure you will know what is going to happen."

"Well, there was a mating ceremony in my old pack just before I was taken." Aden thought hard. "Actually, now I come to think about it there really weren't all that many."

Blaze quirked an eyebrow. "Why am I not surprised?"

Darric shuffled up the bed until he was sitting with his back to the headboard, Aden clutched in his lap. "Our mating ceremony will be a little different. Half of Jefferson pack will be here, White Waters, representatives from Colorado Springs—"

"And the rest," Blaze interrupted, grinning.

Aden stammered, "W-what?"

"It's a big thing. There will be a reception afterwards for the humans while we hunt. We were hoping you could host that. We've invited Senator Mason and a delegation." "Marcus Flint," put in Darric.

Conner leaned over to Aden. "We'd also like you to invite anyone you'd like from your old pack."

Aden's head whirled with the logistics.

Blaze stroked his face. "This has to be a big thing for two reasons. We need to demonstrate our authority to the wolf packs. Many of them are coming to see if Orion's Circle truly has been formed."

"What are you going to do?" Aden asked nervously. He knew enough to know the old mating ceremonies often involved very public coupling. Darric snickered and Blaze chuckled.

"There won't need to be any demonstrations," Conner said. "The power when Orion's Circle is created will be tremendous. All the wolves will know."

"Well, thank God for that," Aden said drily, "and the second reason is to convince the humans, I guess? Show our *baser* personalities can be controlled?"

Conner laughed full out. Blaze got out of bed, and Darric hugged Aden tight.

There was a knock at the door. Conner shrugged his shorts on and went to answer it. They were all seated at the table tucking into breakfast when something occurred to Aden. Blaze answered the question right as Aden thought of it. "Your pack doctor seems to have disappeared."

"So, that's what had you worried this morning?" Aden exclaimed. He knew there had been something.

"We just don't trust him."

Aden looked at Blaze. "No, neither do I. The more I think about it, the more I feel he was really responsible for a lot of what Alpha Richard did."

"The power behind the throne," said Darric as he refilled his coffee thoughtfully.

"Aden, can you remember how long the doctor has been in your pack?" Blaze asked.

Aden shook his head. "He's always been there as far as I know, but Jay's parents would be able to help you with that question." Aden suddenly felt sick. "They're still alive?"

Blaze nodded. "The only wolves that were actually killed were the ones who were fighting, mainly gammas." He looked at his watch. "I have arranged for Jay to visit you this morning, he'll be here in an hour."

Aden smiled. He was pleased. He ignored the low growl from Conner—though he quite liked the thought of him being jealous over Jay. He looked over at the bananas and started peeling one thoughtfully.

Conner smiled. "You hate bananas."

Aden shrugged, he just suddenly fancied one. He could change his mind, couldn't he?

"Jay!" Aden exclaimed as he walked into the common area. Jay sat with his parents around one of the small tables. Small seating groups had been placed around coffee tables. Plants were dotted about and Aden could see Lilly hovering over the serving area that was being designed as an extension of the large kitchen.

"We liked your ideas," Conner murmured as they walked towards the group of three nervous looking people. Aden smiled reassuringly at them—Jay's parents.

Jay grinned and ambled over to meet Aden. His parents hung back, both with equally worried expressions. Aden opened his mouth to greet them but was enveloped in a bear hug from his friend. Aden returned the squeeze.

"God, it is so good to see you."

Jay mussed Aden's hair playfully. "Wasn't sure if you still hugged the commoners, Ade."

"Watch the hair, ginge," Aden said, the same automatic response they'd grown up with, and they both burst out laughing. He glanced towards Jay's parents, satisfied when he saw Conner shaking hands with Jay's dad.

"How are they doing?"

Jay sighed, his freckled face sobering. "Embarrassed. Relieved. Ashamed. Thankful. Worried. Take your pick." He stared at Aden. "You okay, bro?"

Aden smiled. "I'm very okay. Kellan's back with you though, isn't he?"

Jay nodded. "Yeah." He shuffled his feet and glanced down. "Ade—" Aden put a hand on Jay's arm.

"No, not between us. It's forgotten. You're not responsible for your brother."

Jay looked up at Aden. "You're my brother too, always have been."

Aden swallowed the lump in his throat just in time as Conner brought Jay's parents over. Jay's dad cleared his throat. "Omega, can we offer any reparation—"

The smaller man's words were cut off when Aden threw his arms around him. "Carl, it is so good to see you." He reached out. "Ann?"

With a sob, Jay's mom stepped into their huddle. "Aden, honey, we were so worried."

"I wanted to come with your dad to see the Alpha, but the gammas wouldn't let me through," Carl said.

Aden nodded. "I'm glad you didn't, you might have been killed too."

Ann put a shaky hand up to her lips. "Are you happy, Aden? Truly?" She glanced over at Conner, who was leaning back casually on one of the new tables. "You can always come home with us."

Aden smiled and stretched his arm out towards Conner. In a flash Conner held his hand, brought it up to his smiling lips for a kiss, and then Aden was gently but firmly pulled into Conner's side. At the same time, Aden smelled the familiar clean scent of Blaze who came to stand next to Conner. He knew Darric had followed him too.

Carl's eyes rose in shock, and Ann blurted out. "So the rumors are true?"

But before anyone could say anything, Carl took a step away, lowered himself to his knees, and bowed his head. He brought his right hand to his chest. "Alpha's, mine."

Blaze and Conner immediately let go of Aden. With Darric, they took a step forward and copied Carl, then brought their right hands to their chests. "Alpha's, yours," they all repeated solemnly.

Aden felt every hair on the back of his neck rise as Alpha power swirled around the room. Even the wolves constructing the serving area paused and brought their fists to their chests. Blaze took another step forward, clasped Carl's arms, and drew him upright. "I do not need supplicants, Carl. We need partners and friends if we are to grow strong."

Carl nodded. "With all that I am, Alpha."

"What can we do to help?" Ann suddenly found her voice.

Darric stepped forward. "Coffee, anyone?" which brought a few relieved laughs.

Aden wrinkled his nose, but suddenly thought of something. "Ann, does your mom still have breathing problems?"

Ann nodded sadly. "She's in bed most days."

Aden looked at Blaze but Darric was faster and beckoned one of his gammas over. "When Carl and Ann leave, please send the pack doctor with them."

Aden nearly laughed at their astonished looks. Coffee arrived with a beaming Lilly. Aden shuffled a bit further away from the smell.

Ann jumped up delightedly. "Lilly?"

Lilly nearly dropped the cookies she was carrying in shock. "Ann Cantley, as I live and breathe." This of course had everyone laughing again.

Blaze leaned over to Carl. "What condition are your living quarters in over there?"

Carl's face dropped. "Pitiful, Alpha. Anyone who wasn't counted as one of Alpha Richard's inner circle had to exist on what we could grow. Hunting was forbidden. You are aware we were forbidden any contacts with humans or other packs?" Blaze nodded. "We also have my daughter's family with us."

Aden gaped. "With the kids? Where are you all sleeping?" Jay's mom had a cozy two bedroom cottage. Cozy, but old.

"Outside," Jay put in, munching his fifth cookie.

"Carl, we have just finished the first phase of the living quarters here, attached to the main house. We would be pleased to offer your family the chance to live here."

Jay gaped and looked eagerly at his dad.

"Not for free, Alpha," Carl blustered.

"Indeed not." Conner smiled, and nodded to where Lilly was eagerly showing Ann the new kitchen set up. "I think your wife may already have a job."

"Carl's a teacher, an incredibly good one," Aden said excitedly. He remembered his own "secret" lessons the Alpha hadn't approved of. Richard had always said you didn't need math to be able to hunt. Carl had always whispered to him, *but how would you know how many rabbits to catch to feed everyone?*

"Excellent." Blaze stood and Carl copied. He put out his large hand. "We are going to need a school."

Chapter Sixteen

Aden wasn't nervous, he was flat out terrified. Large delegations had been arriving all day from various packs. His hand had been shaken so many times it was sore, and his head was pounding. In fact, if he hadn't known the pack doctor had gone with Jay's dad, he would have been tempted to see him. Or at least see if anyone had some aspirin. He'd managed to dodge everyone and had come to lie down for a little while, but the nerves in his stomach wouldn't quit long enough for him to get some sleep.

"I wondered where you'd disappeared to."

Aden sighed at Darric's voice, and tried to burrow his head in the pillow. He felt a hand stroke his back. "What's the matter?"

Aden moaned; the hand had been so soothing. Now, if Darric would just reach a little higher. *Oh*. Aden dissolved as fingers spread into the hair on the back of his neck, and another hand twisted the stubborn knot in his shoulders.

"Mmm," Aden replied.

Darric chuckled. He bent and followed his fingers with his lips, lightly pressing up and down Aden's spine. Aden wasn't moving, in fact it was highly unlikely anything short of a nuclear attack would have gotten him to move at this point.

"Have you eaten?"

"I ate with you," Aden just managed to speak.

He could feel Darric's frown. "Aden, that was nearly seven hours ago, and you were sick again this morning."

"I'm not hungry, just tired."

Darric sighed. "We have at least an hour before the reception and the bonding. Close your eyes."

Aden did, but there was something that was bothering him. "Darric?"

"Yes, my beautiful Aden?"

Aden smiled, he loved it when Darric called him beautiful, made him feel like he was. "The bonding. I mean, how?" Aden could feel pink stealing over his cheeks and was glad his head was buried. "I thought we'd bonded, I mean..."

Darric chuckled. "We started the bonding process, and kind of got interrupted as I recall." Aden blushed harder, and Darric smiled. "I'm sorry, I shouldn't tease." He took a breath. "Yes, you will make love to Blaze, but it will have to be after the bonding ceremony." Darric nibbled on the back of Aden's neck. "I'm quite jealous, but I intend to make use of every day of the next six hundred years to catch up."

Aden smiled. God, he was lucky. He thought about the ceremony. "I've seen a mating ritual." He hesitated on the words. In the ritual he's seen, both weres had been forced to bond out in the open for all to see. It hadn't been about making love, it had been about entertainment for the Alpha.

Darric shook his head. "All the mating rituals I have ever seen were beautiful, and nothing happens in public that should be private. It's not embarrassing, Aden." Darric's hand smoothed the back of his head and some of the tension dissolved. "We call upon Sirius to bless Orion's Circle." Darric frowned. "Actually, seeing as how we are the first ever Orion's Circle, I'm not a hundred percent sure what will happen, but neither Blaze nor Connor are worried."

Aden grunted. With Darric rubbing the tension out of his neck, speech was impossible. "I'm going to let you sleep for a while, then you're going to have some food."

Aden felt a kiss on the back of his neck, then he didn't feel anything else.

"Aden, beautiful. Wake up."

Aden opened his eyes blearily to Darric. "But you said you'd give me an hour." He'd only just closed his eyes.

He heard Blaze's chuckle. "You've had nearly two. The reception has started. I'm sorry, we can't leave you any longer."

Grumbling, Aden sat up and swung both legs out of bed. He went to stand up, but a sick feeling of giddiness kept him down. He was sure he was going to be sick again. He clutched the hand that was nearest to him.

"Aden, sweetheart, what is it?" Conner pushed his way past Blaze and Darric.

Aden didn't shake his head. He wasn't sure it was a good idea to move anything quickly. He cracked an eye open. Darric brought him some water, and there was a knock at the door.

Blaze opened it to the doctor. Aden grumbled again, wondering how he'd got here so fast.

Darric stood aside to let the doctor near. "Let him help, Aden."

"Alphas, I was just coming to see you all actually," the doctor tutted to himself and started drawing empty vials out of his bag. "Let's do a couple more blood tests, see if the nausea settles down over the weekend. If not, we'll run some different tests."

Even Aden caught the hesitation in the doctor's voice.

He looked at Blaze. "Alpha, I'm sure it's nothing to worry about." He smiled at Aden indulgently. "Your body, even with shifter strength, has had to put up with a lot in the last few months. It may be it needs longer to recover."

"I'll cancel tonight." Blaze looked distraught.

"Absolutely not." Aden declared hotly. All those people? No way.

"I don't need to shift, Blaze," Conner said. "It doesn't ride me as hard as you two."

Blaze looked at Conner, concerned. "Of all of us, you need to shift the most." He held his hand up, "And yes, I know you can do it anytime, but you know the strength a full moon shift gives you."

"Let's wait and see," Conner said. We can always shift briefly and take turns."

Aden wanted to protest but the doctor stuck a thermometer in his mouth.

The doctor smirked. "The Alphas have ordered all new equipment for the clinic, but it hasn't arrived yet."

Aden coughed and sipped some water after the doctor had pronounced his temperature normal—well for a shifter anyway, since it ran a little higher than humans.

Aden stood carefully and smiled. "I feel fine. The faster we go down and do this, the faster it will be over." Blaze growled, but Darric went and fetched his clothes.

Conner helped Aden into some more black dress pants and a teal shirt. "You look amazing." He kissed Aden on the nose. Aden looked around and spied the bowl of fruit, snagging a banana.

He looked up at the silence. "But you want me to eat something," he protested quietly amused. All this fussing would probably get old, well say in around a hundred years, but he was enjoying every second of it at the moment.

He followed Blaze, flanked by Darric and Conner to the entrance hallway. There had been marquees set up outside because even that large space wasn't big enough to hold all the wolves attending from the nearby packs. Aden smiled when he saw Senator Mason talking to Marcus Flint. The guy was dressed casually in jeans and an open-necked blue shirt. Aden spied Jay and his parents; he stiffened when he saw Kellan standing behind them with his head down.

Conner whispered to him. "Blaze wanted to gut him, but we thought you would want Carl and Ann to be happy."

Aden smiled. Conner was right. And he was more embarrassed than mad. "Come with me?"

Aden didn't wait for the reply. He saw Blaze talking to Senator Mason, but he knew damn well Blaze knew where he was heading.

Jay grinned and opened his mouth, but then his smile faltered as he saw Aden's gaze was trained on his brother. Conner stopped to shake Carl's hand and to chat with Ann, but Aden knew he could hear every word.

"Kellan."

The man's bruised, blue-gray eyes lifted in his pale face. The cuts on his lip were still not healed, meaning he hadn't shifted. He flushed slightly and trained his eyes back on the floor. "Omega."

If Aden hadn't been concentrating, he wouldn't have heard the mumbled word. "Kellan, it's Aden, Ade if you like. That's what you used to call me when Jay and I trailed around after you and your friends for all those summers. You were good to me for a lot of years, I don't want some psycho ruining that. He's taken enough from me already." Aden placed his hand on his old friend's arm. "I'm gonna need all the friends I can get."

Kellan hesitated, then covered Aden's hand with his own. "When you've a minute, there are some more things I think the Alphas should know."

"Group hug!" Jay nearly squealed and threw an arm around them both. Aden laughed and then smelled Blaze before he heard him.

"I need you," Blaze said when he drew close enough. Aden nodded, and followed Blaze. Darric snagged his hand and Conner followed them.

The marquee was huge. All the food and drink were laid on long tables, but it was open at one end nearest the trees. A large dais had been built and that was where Blaze headed.

Aden gulped. He didn't like the thought of all these people looking at him. He felt a warm hand on his back and took comfort in realizing it was Conner's touch.

He kept hold of Darric's hand as they climbed the steps onto the platform. Blaze took a step forward. Aden wondered for a second if he was going to need a microphone but when the low, booming voice of his Alpha started, he realized that wasn't necessary.

"Thank you everyone for coming, you are most welcome. To the wolf shifters and to the humans present tonight, this represents the start of something good in this world."

Blaze paused at the smattering of polite applause.

"Too much has been forgotten of our history. Tonight that wrong will start to be put right."

Aden glanced at Conner. He'd tuned out the natural nerves from all of them a while ago, but he felt the spike of confusion and suspicion in the man, and wondered what he was feeling. Conner's eyes were trained on the far left corner of the marquee. Aden wasn't surprised though, it was going to take more than a few words to combat centuries of mistrust.

"Friends, many centuries ago the goddess Sirius created the first wolf in her own image. The idea was that the animal would be a companion to the human hunter, but the experiment didn't work. Humans mistrusted the animal, were afraid of its superior skills, felt it was in competition for the same meat, and eventually the animal turned feral."

Aden saw some of the older wolves, including Carl and Ann, nod in agreement.

"Sirius tried one more time and created wolf shifters. She felt a human appearance would make communication easier between the two species, the shifters blessed with superior strength, speed, and smell. The experiment failed again. This time, it was the fault of the wolves who distrusted the humans and were too busy arguing for dominance within their own ranks to be of any help to our human friends."

Blaze paused, and nodded to Darric. Aden suddenly realized what he was going to do. Darric was the only one of them that could shift back fully clothed, and Conner wasn't strong enough. Quick shifts often took a lot of energy.

Darric stepped up. Blaze continued. "For our human friends, this is so they can see a shift. Our wolves will understand what they are seeing and will need no explanation."

Just as Blaze finished talking the air shimmered in front of Darric, and in an instant a huge silver wolf stood there. Aden could hear gasps and appreciative murmurs from the humans. He even saw one or two of them take a good step back. Darric lifted his head and howled; Aden felt the nerves ramp up in the marquee.

Blaze chuckled. "He's saying hello." Aden smiled at the answering laughter from the crowd.

Blaze turned and nodded to Darric, and in seconds Darric shifted back to a fully clothed human. This time the gasps came from the wolves. One or two of them even dropped to their knees.

Blaze raised his hands. "Friends, to continue with my story, because Sirius's second attempt had failed also, the Gods were furious at what they deemed her interference in human affairs. She was banished, her everlasting punishment that she be recreated as a star so she could shine down and see eternally how her experiments at bettering the human race had failed.

"But she was granted a final request—that one day, when humans could accept and embrace the differences between one another, Orion's Circle would be formed." Blaze took a step forward. "That day, my friends, has finally come."

Aden grinned at the cheering that rose from the packs. He'd spied Jay pushing himself forward—the guy was doing as much hollering as ten people together.

A prickle of unease climbed over Aden's skin, and he immediately glanced at Conner. Conner looked worried, and Aden felt his worry.

"I would like to invite Senator Mason up to say a few words, and then we will begin the bonding ceremony and the hunt."

Conner ignored Blaze, who was still speaking, and stepped behind him to whisper to Aden. "You can feel something, can't you?"

"I can feel it in you. What's wrong?"

Conner shrugged and shook his head, "I don't—"

Conner shut his mouth abruptly, just as Aden heard murmurs rise from the crowd. Blaze and Senator Mason turned to the left like everyone else as the sound of helicopter blades filled the clearing. Blaze nodded to his gammas and they spread out along both sides of the dais.

Three huge helicopters appeared in the distance. To Aden they looked like flying busses. More worrying were the large guns apparent on either side of each one. All three landed gracefully in the clearing to the left. Before Blaze even had the chance to tell people to calm down, talking and shouting erupted from the left side of the marquee and a group of people started moving forward. To Aden's complete horror, from the corner of the crowd, Senator Addison led a group of armed men including the pack doctor, Gregory Madden.

The stupid woman was shouting as she walked. Soldiers streamed out of each helicopter, and within seconds the whole marquee was surrounded with armed men.

Blaze put a hand up to his gammas to stand down before things got ugly.

"Senator Mason, I tried to get ahold of you earlier to warn you against coming here today," Senator Addison said, stepping onto the dais.

"What is the meaning of this?" The furious man stepped forward.

"Ladies and gentlemen, you must listen to me." Unlike Blaze, Senator Addison had brought a microphone. "The terrifying discovery I have made today pertains to the safety of the werewolves as well as all humankind." An abstract part of Aden wondered why, if the woman was so terrified, she had still managed to put on the god-awful red lipstick.

"I have discovered that a large group of werewolves have been experimenting with immortality. They intend to enslave all humanity. I even have a werewolf doctor here who was so disgusted with his superiors he escaped."

Aden stepped forward, furious, but he was beaten to it by Darric.

"That is partly true," Darric said. "However, you will find that it was the doctor himself that was responsible for those experiments. We have many witnesses here that will testify to that. That group has been disbanded and there will be no more experiments of any kind."

Aden relaxed. Everyone could hear the sincerity in Darric's voice, and everything would be all right.

The Senator smiled, and Aden didn't know how he wasn't suddenly sick. He'd seen that type of smile so many times in the past year—that moment when someone knew something you didn't and it was going to be very bad.

"Indeed," boomed the Senator. "Will you promise to answer a question, honestly and truthfully, to demonstrate your sincerity and show the humans you mean no harm?"

Darric smiled. Conner shook his head frantically. Aden didn't know how his legs were still holding him up.

The Senator smiled again, looked straight at Blaze, and raised the microphone. "How old are you?"

Chapter Seventeen

Aden didn't know how it was possible for complete silence to descend with so many people there, but nonetheless it seemed like the birds even held their breath. Darric looked at Blaze helplessly.

"As you can see, Senator Mason, the very fact that this creature won't answer testifies to their lying."

Senator Mason looked at Blaze doubtfully. "What is she implying? How old are you?"

Blaze opened his mouth, but Senator Addison carried on. "The wolves have made it plain that they want to be trained by *our* military, ostensibly to fight terrorism side by side, but Ladies and Gentleman, it is clear to everyone their real reason is to learn our weapon and technology secrets, to steal from this great country of ours. The real danger of terrorism isn't from some savages that live in other countries, it's the ones that live in our back yards."

Aden could hear crying from the children present as the groups of werewolves were surrounded. The soldiers raised their guns in answer to the chorus of voices that broke out.

Darric tried again to speak soothingly, but soldiers had climbed onto the dais and guns were now being trained on all of them.

"Calm down everyone," carried on the Senator triumphantly. "We have found out their nefarious plans and have a solution. As you can see from the different packs represented today, this problem reaches far and wide. Your government will introduce registration for all wolf shifters. They will be detained in specialized camps until we are satisfied they won't be a danger to anyone."

Conner trembled. "Dear God, some madman tried that already in 1939." Even Senator Mason paled at that.

Aden looked back at the crowd, hearing some shouting. Some of the younger wolves were panicking. *Oh God.* Two of them had shifted. Jay stood trying to calm down the soldier who was pointing a gun at the bigger one. It was too close to the full moon for the younger ones to be able to control their shift. Another boy crouched and turned into a small brown wolf, hackles raised, teeth snapping.

Another soldier raised his gun as the wolf crouched, ready to pounce. Hysterical voices rose up, Blaze shouted in warning, someone screamed, and at the same time as a gun shot rang out, Blaze leaped through the air, shifting as he did into the beautiful, black creature Aden knew him to be.

Aden screamed in warning as bullets hit Blaze's fur. Darric tried to shift but had the barrel of a gun pushed into his face. Conner was pinned down. Blaze landed with a thud on his side, the ground shaking as he hit it. His black sides heaved once then stilled.

Conner screamed and collapsed. "Blaze!"

Aden looked at where Darric struggled, tears streaming down his face. Aden couldn't speak, he couldn't think. It was finished, over. Agony ripped through him; as he'd seen that black body breathe its last, he wanted to join it.

The gammas were helpless to stop the soldiers herding the weres into groups. The young male adults were being steadily separated. To Aden's disgust the teenagers that had shifted were being held in chains. Screams and shouts rose above the cacophony of voices, and more than one soldier raised his weapon as another youngster shifted. Aden swung his head back to the Senator, ready to beg, and caught sight of the Senator standing with Madden.

This time it wasn't helplessness that robbed his voice and stilled his body. It wasn't sorrow, and it wasn't misery.

Each of them turned to Aden with the same evil, satisfied smile. The doctor mouthed the words, "Welcome home, little omega."

Aden stilled. He felt the hate swirl around him, knew it was directing the actions of the crowd. Hate, fear, mistrust. Aden recognized them all, because he had grown up with them all his life, helpless to do anything about them. But not now. Aden knew what he had to do. He knew exactly what he had to do. He blessed his small stature for the first time in his life, because none of the gammas had attempted to restrain him. Aden stepped to the edge of the dais, the confusion and shouting raging all around him, stretched out his arms, and opened his mind.

Listen to me.

He stumbled from the sudden onslaught of fear and hatred that hit him.

Listen to me.

No, No Conner begged, *Aden. Stop, you can't take on everyone's emotions, it's dangerous. There's too many of them...I can't lose you too.*

Aden sent out a resigned smile to Conner, and looked once more at the still, fur body that lay on the ground. Someone else had given everything for mankind, because Blaze had a vision that one day everyone would be at peace with one another, love would be celebrated, differences embraced. If there was one last thing he could do, it was this.

Listen to me.

One by one Aden took everything. Hate, fear, jealousy, distrust, anger, contempt, loathing—and the one that hurt him the most, apathy, because caring too much was better than not caring at all.

The pain sent him to his knees, but even then when his lungs screamed for the oxygen that his overworked system could no longer process, he kept his arms outstretched, the sound of the guns dropping to the floor and the cries quieting, the sweetest music he had ever heard. Finally, his muscles screamed in protest and he dropped his arms, unable to keep them extended to welcome the approaching blackness he knew would soon shut off the pain exploding in his head.

Chapter Eighteen

Aden, Aden.

He knew he was dreaming. His mom's voice sounded so real. Heaven? He hoped.

Omega.

Aden's eyes snapped open. His mom wouldn't call him that. He sat up quickly, and looked around. He was lying on the grass, in a clearing he recognized from being a child. Confused, he turned to the sound of the voice. A small golden wolf lay in the grass sunning itself, looking for all the world like it was supposed to be there, panting steadily and licking its front paw. Aden sat up and looked around. There wasn't another soul in sight.

He glanced back at the wolf, feeling incredibly foolish. "Did you just talk to me?"

Of course, omega.

Aden gaped and scrambled back as the air in front of the wolf shimmered and a woman with gray hair and a long white dress stood in the wolf's place.

"Who—what, I mean—"

The woman smiled and held a hand up to silence Aden. "Peace, omega." Aden decided he'd better be standing, so he stood quickly. "I am Sirius."

Aden gaped in awe and wondered if he should bow or something.

The woman smiled. "Omega, it is not necessary to bow. In fact—" Sirius glanced upwards. "Mmm, maybe not."

"But, I thought you were a star." Aden cringed. Of all the things he should have said, that definitely wasn't one of them. He was talking to a God, he should...a shard of pain pierced him along with the memory of his beautiful...Blaze. *Blaze*. Aden sank to his knees. "Please—"

But his words were silenced as Sirius laid a finger on his lips. "Do get up, child, it may still be quite damp down there." Aden shook his head, totally confused. Maybe he'd died, maybe this was some sort of test. He glanced around suspiciously, barely noticing she had gently pulled him upright.

"Now, we haven't much time. Listen carefully." She raised her eyes upwards a little. "My err...*colleagues* were so impressed with your selfless act of a few minutes ago, I get another chance, and that, my dear omega, means you do too. I will send you back, but I can only give you an hour at the most."

Aden blinked.

"And this is very important, omega. I can only do this once so whatever happens this time cannot be undone. Do you understand?" Aden gazed wordlessly.

"Omega, do you understand? I can never, ever do this again." She let go of his arms and smoothed her hair in place.

Aden struggled to process what he was being told. "An hour? How? I mean, what do I do?"

Sirius smiled. "Blaze will know."

Aden's heart slammed in his chest so hard it felt like a rib had cracked along with it. "Blaze?" *Oh*. "*Blaze?*" Aden repeated incredulously. "He's okay? Truly?"

Sirius nodded impatiently. "Well, at least for another hour anyway."

Aden wanted to laugh hysterically. Completely forgetting this regal woman was a goddess, he stepped up to her and flung his arms around her waist. "Thank you, thank you so much."

He felt her patting his head. "Thank you, little omega, and make sure you get your physician to examine you tomorrow, that's very important. Chop chop." Sirius made a shooing move with her hands. She looked heavenward in frustration when Aden didn't move. "Osiris, you haven't got the new colloquialisms correct at all, the boy has no idea what I am saying." Aden closed his eyes.

"Aden, beautiful. Wake up."

He opened his eyes blearily to Darric. "But you said you'd give me an hour." He'd only just closed his eyes. He... "Blaze!" Aden scrambled to try and get out of bed. "Blaze!" He almost shrieked when the big guy emerged from the bathroom.

He flung his arms around him, causing Blaze to take a step back. "I'm going to let you have more naps, beautiful, if that's how—"

"You were *dead.*" Aden cried, nearly beside himself.

"Hush Aden, you must have been dreaming."

Aden turned to Conner. "This is really important and I haven't much time."

Darric grinned. "Well, just enough to put clothes on—"

Listen to me. The words had the effect he wanted. All three Alphas subsided. He closed his eyes to let them in. *I just met Sirius.*

When Aden opened his eyes, he saw three identical shocked faces. "There's more." He closed his eyes again and played the part back on the dais in his mind. It was like a horror movie.

When he opened his eyes this time they were wet. Blaze shook his head, Darric reached out for Aden, and Conner paled. Aden squeezed Darric's fingers. "There's no time."

Blaze pushed himself away from the wall. "Aden's right, we have to move quickly." He strode to the door and spoke to the gamma that was stationed outside. "Please escort Senator Mason's party to the small meeting room downstairs, serve them refreshments."

Blaze turned to Darric. "Reposition the gammas, get Hunter's gammas to help. Prevent the Senator getting to the dais. Detain the doctor as soon as he is found. Conner, get Ben to organize moving the teens and the children to the large meeting room. Lilly and Ann will help, I want them out of the way."

Conner and Darric both shot Aden a loving look and disappeared. Blaze turned to Aden, and held out his hand. "Omega, we have a senator to convince."

Aden clasped Blaze's hand tightly. "The helicopters, don't forget the helicopters," he urged.

Blaze paused for one second and held Aden's gaze. He reached a hand up and smoothed Aden's hair away from his eyes. "You humble me. I have never met anyone who is prepared to give so much of themselves selflessly for other people." He bent and brushed a kiss on Aden's cheek.

Aden smiled. "Why? You've been doing that for six hundred years." He clasped Blaze's hand as they hurried out. "I'm just playing catch-up."

Blaze and Aden went hurriedly down to the small meeting room. They passed the entrance area and saw Lilly and Debbie just coming up the steps with some of the kids. Aden smiled as he heard Lilly speaking to the kids. He would like to disappear and have cake too.

Blaze and Aden strode into the meeting room just as Senator Mason and his colleagues arrived as well.

The senator shook hands with them both. "Quite the party."

Blaze smiled. "Senator, we need your help."

"Has this got anything to do with the phone call I just got from...?"

Blaze sighed. "You need to know—"

The door banged open and Terry stood there. "Alpha, apologies—"

Blaze cut Terry off as he shot out of the door. Rapid gunfire could be heard coming from outside. Aden ran after Blaze. This was wrong, it hadn't been an hour. What the hell was happening?

Something must have happened to change things.

Aden gasped when he got outside. Complete silence had settled over the marquee. Soldiers had appeared from somewhere, there were no helicopters. Guns were trained on Blaze's gammas. There was a crowd of people huddled together, and Aden heard the hiss from Blaze at the same as time he heard a woman sobbing.

Grief slammed into Aden, and he pushed his way through. *Oh, God no.*

Before Aden even saw the red hair he knew who was lying on the ground. Darric was crouched helplessly next to a sobbing Ann. The pack doctor rushed over to help.

Hate. Fear. Anguish. Guilt. Aden was swamped with them all as another shout ran out. He looked up to the noise, and people scurried to get out of the way.

"Nobody moves. I will rip out her throat before any of you can pull your triggers." Kellan stood holding the Senator captive. He had partially shifted and his claws were causing rivulets of blood to run down her neck. "Tell them. Tell them what you did."

The Senator shook, could hardly get words out of a strangled throat. "I didn't do anything—"

"Liar!" screamed Kellan. "It was you. You funded the labs. Tell them." He poked his claws harder at the Senator's throat.

"Kellan." Aden spoke quietly, but he knew everyone could hear him. "If she tells us, will you let her go? You don't want to be responsible for causing your mom more pain." He nodded to where Ann was sobbing over Jay's motionless body. Kellan held his breath. He knew Senator Mason was talking hastily on the phone to someone and he had to buy them all time. Senator Addison wasn't likely to confess to anything if she thought she was dead anyway.

Senator Mason stepped up beside Aden. He made a lowering motion with his hand and some of the gun barrels dropped a little. "Senator, what is the meaning of all this, what labs does the young man mean?"

"Remember, I know if you are truthful," Aden added. He couldn't be exactly sure—they needed Conner to be sure—but Senator Addison didn't know that.

Kellan relaxed his arm around the Senator's neck a little so she could speak.

"You're all fools," she spat the words out. "I'm doing this for the good of our country."

"Doing exactly what for the good of our country?" asked the Senator in a reasonable voice.

Her eyes gleamed. "They have superior speed and strength. They can detect IED's by smell alone for Christ's sake. We need them, all of them. Not just a few in specialized units." Aden watched in disgust as the woman carried on. "The doctor is developing a way of controlling them. Just imagine super soldiers that are controlled by one Alpha that we control. There won't be any problems with the chain of command, no worries that one Alpha's order will countermand someone else's." She leaned forward triumphantly, ignoring the knife pressing against her. "They will do exactly what we say, when we say it."

Senator Mason raised a disbelieving eyebrow. "And how can you be assured that we will be able to control that one Alpha who controls all the wolves?"

Senator Addison hesitated. Kellan growled and tightened his hold once more. "Tell him, bitch, tell him exactly what you and Madden are doing."

The Senator tried to swallow, but choked. Aden took a little of Kellan's anger into himself, and winced slightly.

Aden? Aden glanced at Blaze's concerned blue eyes.

I'm okay. To his relief, Kellan's arm slackened slightly.

"We agreed to fund his experiments," she acknowledged reluctantly.

"But Alpha Richard and his son are both dead," Blaze said. "I doubt if anyone else has such complicated ambitions."

Aden nearly smiled at how reasonable Blaze sounded. Blaze knew exactly where he was leading the conversation, and he knew exactly who was really interested in immortality.

"Who is interested in becoming Alpha of the werewolves, Senator?" Mason asked slowly, obviously understanding where Blaze's question was heading.

The Senator made a strangled sound in her throat and a little more blood appeared along the edge of Kellan's claws.

"It's the doctor, isn't it? Gregory Madden," Aden said slowly. The Senator gave a defeated slump and nodded.

"Okay, son," Senator Mason addressed Kellan. "Let her go. We've got what we need."

"Not yet." Conner said, running towards them. "She isn't telling us every reason she has for forcing conscription."

Senator Mason moved nearer. "Actually, she doesn't have to. I've just been informed she had powerful family links to Alko Aerospace that she has never acknowledged."

"Alko?" murmured Aden, confused. His head was throbbing.

The senator nodded. "Alko Aerospace already has the initial designs made for werewolf body armor. They would be given the contract if wolves were forcibly conscripted, and there is no way they could know about this unless someone told them." The Senator glared at Addison. "It will make the struggling company millions."

Aden was stunned. All this? All this because of money?

Kellan was sweating, furiously shaking his head. "She's killed my brother."

Soldiers raised their guns all around them, pointing at Kellan. "Kellan, no one else needs to die today," Aden said, sadly.

Listen to me. Aden shook as he felt the bitterness enter his system. He saw Blaze move out of the corner of his eye. So much anger, so much sorrow. Aden could feel the blackness at the edge of his mind. He knew it was too much, on top of what he'd asked his body earlier.

Listen to me.

Aden couldn't let Kellan die. There had been enough death. He vaguely saw the hand with which Kellan held the senator slacken, knew it was working. He pushed to open his mind to a little more pain.

"Aden, stop. You're not strong enough for this." Blaze's words, low and desperate, registered. Aden looked at Kellan's puzzled face. He could do this, he was nearly there.

Listen to me.

"Aden, stop. For God's sake stop." Blaze's voice was lower, more urgent, desperate.

Blaze caught his arm. *I forbid you. Stop.*

Aden stepped away from Blaze, and flung his arms wide. *Listen to me.*

He heard the knife drop as blackness descended. The last thing he felt was Blaze's arms catching him.

Epilogue

Aden woke up suddenly, gasping. Firm arms held him close. "Aden, shh...it's fine, everything's fine."

Aden let out a shuddering breath as Conner's words registered.

"Kellan?" *Jay.* He squeezed his eyes shut tight. "Jay."

"He's fine. The doctor got him stable enough and Blaze made him shift." Conner grinned mischievously. "Hurts like hell when an Alpha compels a wolf to shift, but it healed him."

Aden sank back into Conner's arms, the rush of relief incredible. He didn't even bother saying he didn't know Alphas could compel wolves to shift. Something else that had been wrong in his old pack. He heard a noise and opened his eyes fully. The pack doctor stood nearby, next to Blaze, smiling benevolently. Blaze looked white as a sheet, and angry, incredibly angry.

Aden felt a spark of alarm and sat up. "What is it?" Had the last time he had taken emotions damaged him?

Darric looked a little pale also, but when he glanced at Conner, Conner had a huge grin on his face.

Before anyone had a chance to speak, a wave of nausea rolled over Aden, and he felt sweat break out on his forehead. *Oh God.*

"The water, quick." Conner beckoned Darric, who sat nearest the table. Conner held the glass. "Small sips." Aden hardly dared opened his mouth, wondering how fast he could get to the bathroom. "Cloth." Conner nodded to Blaze, and Blaze hurried to the bathroom. In a few seconds Aden had a wonderful, cool cloth pressed against the back of his neck. "Take a few deep breaths, gorgeous." Aden closed his eyes, and did. Miraculously, the nausea abated a little.

"My wife recommends keeping a few salty crackers by the bed." The doctor chuckled. "Apparently it helps if she could manage a few before she sits up."

Aden cracked an eye open in confusion at the doctor's words. "What?"

The doctor chuckled again. "I'll leave you to it, Alphas. Call me with anything, and I'll be by tomorrow."

The door closed behind the doctor and Darric sat on the opposite side of the bed from Conner. Conner was still smiling; Blaze was pacing up and down the room.

Aden sighed. "Is someone going to tell me what's wrong?"

"There's nothing wrong, gorgeous." Conner patted his arm.

Blaze snorted. "How can you say that?"

Aden squirmed and Conner gave Blaze a black look. "Blaze, for God's sake, you're scaring him."

Blaze stopped his pacing, and turned to the door. "I'm going to see if the gammas have everything cleared away." Everyone winced as the door slammed behind him.

"What did I do this time?" Aden asked desolately. It was never going to work. He'd known from the start he wasn't going to be good enough for Blaze. "Is everyone all right...Kellan?"

Conner smiled. "Yes, everyone's fine." He encouraged Aden to take another sip. "Better?"

Aden nodded. His stomach had settled, it was his heart that was giving him the most trouble at the moment. He slid down the bed, and Conner came with him. Aden glanced at Darric and saw the worried look pass between him and Conner. He swallowed heavily. "Are you going to tell me what's wrong?" He wasn't sure he wanted to know.

Conner rubbed his arm. Darric drew feather light circles on his chest. Aden sighed and closed his eyes. So good.

"There's nothing wrong, Aden, you're not sick, and Blaze isn't mad," Darric put in hurriedly. "Well, he is, but not at you."

"Our pack doctor comes from a long line of healers. In England, sometime in the middle ages, his great, great, whatever"—Conner grinned—"started taking note of some of the medical legends associated with werewolves. He wanted to know why weres could heal by shifting, and if that gift could be used to help some of the thousands dying from the plague. It couldn't, as you know—Sirius only granted that gift to shifters—but he was puzzled with your symptoms and decided to look and see if there were any old records of the powerful omegas in history that suffered anything similar."

"Powerful?" Aden smiled, half asleep.

"The omega always ruled at the right hand of the Alpha, often as mates."

"Often the same sex," added Darric.

"It's no wonder omegas are becoming rare then," Aden replied.

"They aren't rare because they weren't being born, Aden. They were being abused and mistreated. Omegas stopped declaring themselves through fear. There were recorded cases of suicide." Aden nodded sadly. He knew, he remembered what it had felt like.

Darric dropped a kiss on Aden's head, and repeated Conner's words. "They weren't rare because they weren't being born, Aden."

Aden opened his eyes, "But you just told me a lot of Alpha-omega pairings were the same sex. Of course that would cause a drop in population." He laughed, then paused when neither of his Alphas laughed with him.

Aden blinked slowly. "Conner, tell me." Aden pushed Darric's hand away. "What exactly is wrong with me?" His heart was pounding.

"You're pregnant, Aden."

Even when Conner said the words he was afraid he was going to hear, Aden shook his head in disbelief. "That's...impossible."

Darric clasped his arm gently. "It's true Aden, there have been recorded incidences of it, just not in the last few centuries."

Aden glanced down unbelievingly at his still flat stomach. "I don't believe you."

Conner smiled. "Yes, you do. You know we would never lie to you. The doc got the blood tests back. Blaze is going to pay for an ultrasound for the clinic so we can see."

Aden shook his head, stunned. "Th-that's impossible," he protested, weakly. "I mean. How?" He'd never seen a baby being born, but he knew for a fact he didn't have the right body parts. "How—I mean where?"

Darric paled, but Connor chuckled, eyes shining. "The doctor says there is documented evidence of the body altering to accommodate the baby."

Aden almost smiled at Conner's excitement, almost. "You're smiling, but Blaze was angry." He'd seen Blaze's face.

Conner lifted his hand to kiss it. "It's wonderful, Aden. Blaze isn't angry. He feels helpless. I told you he doesn't do well with things out of his control. He worries for you, he's worried that we ask too much of you."

"The last time you diffused Kellan's emotions, Blaze..." Darric looked helplessly at Conner.

"He forbid me. Like I was a child." Resentment burned through Aden. "It's the only thing I've ever been able to do, and he said I couldn't."

"He's an Alpha, sweetie. An incredibly powerful one, and the one person he wanted to protect he couldn't."

"Because a certain stubborn omega insisted on doing something that could hurt him. *Again*," Darric added with exasperation, and Conner cupped Aden's chin.

Aden leaned into the hand. He loved Conner with all his heart, and as he felt Darric's hand rest gently on his shoulder, he knew he loved Darric just as much. He was secretly thrilled about the baby. Confused, scared, worried—all of that—but thrilled. He didn't believe what Conner said about Blaze though, the baby was just something else to worry about to add to Blaze's long list. Would he resent them both eventually? Could he stay knowing that?

He sat up. He wanted to see Jay, and looked at his Alphas. He reached out with his mind, and sighed, frustrated. "He's turned it off again, hasn't he?"

Conner sighed. "Yes, stubborn fool. I hate not having you in my head."

Darric chuckled. "The bonding will have to wait for the next full moon unfortunately, then he won't be able to shut us out, no matter how much he sulks."

Aden thought. There was no way either of them were going to let him out of their sight to see Jay. He lay back slowly and yawned.

Conner patted his arm. "You should rest."

Darric stood. "We're going to help Blaze. There's a lot of clearing up to do. Senator Mason is still here talking to Blaze and Hunter. Aden nodded, eyes shut. He couldn't...couldn't look at them. Not just now.

"Conner," whispered Darric. He obviously thought Aden was nearly asleep. The bed dipped and rose as Conner stood. Aden heard them whispering together as they both left.

Aden got up and blindly threw some clothes on. As he quickly pulled down a polo shirt, the damp collar brushed his wet face. Wet? Aden sat helplessly. Where was he going to go? He didn't want to go anywhere. He loved his three big Alphas with every fiber of his being, totally, completely. Just...why? Why did love have to hurt this much? He brushed another tear angrily from his face. He couldn't be what they needed, he'd never been good at anything, and now? Now, he'd found something he could do. He'd help build a better world. Aden shook his head sadly, but Blaze didn't even want him to do that. He couldn't stay. They could still bond with someone else.

Aden bit his lip furiously. He wasn't staying where he wasn't valued.

The door crashed open, and Aden jumped. Blaze padded into the room, fully shifted, black sides heaving, fur shaking, blue eyes gleaming.

God, he is so beautiful.

Before Aden could even react, Blaze shifted back, completely naked, blue eyes still gleaming wickedly, cock jutting up so hard it looked like it could cut diamonds. If Aden had any spit in his dry mouth he would have swallowed. He just whimpered.

"Never, ever"—Blaze advanced slowly—"think, for one single second"—he bent and drew Aden up against his chest—"that I don't want"—Blaze cupped his face and bent his head—"you." He pulled at Aden's lower lip with his teeth. "Every damn second, of every day."

Blaze's mouth closed over Aden's, capturing the moan that had accompanied him being held tightly against Blaze's length. Aden shivered as he felt Blaze's cock push into his pants. The door slammed again as a silver wolf careered into the room, sending a coffee table flying, closely followed by a golden brown one.

Aden looked up, startled, breathless. "I thought you were in meetings. Did you go out for a run?"

Darric shifted immediately and righted the table. Conner was a second or two behind him, panting. "Blaze, never do that again." He clutched his chest grinning. "Can wolves get heart attacks?"

Aden glanced back at Blaze, who had a faint pink tinge to his face. Realization washed over him. "You haven't turned your thoughts off at all, have you? You knew I was going to leave—you heard me."

Conner raised his eyebrows. "Sneaky devil. How long have you been able to do that?" Aden was stunned. Blaze had turned everyone else's thoughts off, but kept his own link open.

Blaze wrapped an arm around Aden. "Never mind me, our little omega was plotting his escape."

Aden stood back and nearly stamped his foot. "That's it, that's just what I mean. I'm not little." Aden was nearly shouting. "I'm normal height. Just because you three are the size of houses doesn't make me small." Aden trailed off, his voice quieter as all three Alphas regarded him in astonishment. "It doesn't make me less than you three." He looked at Blaze. "I was treated as garbage for a long time, don't you make me feel inferior as well." Aden's voice nearly gave out on the last word.

Blaze sighed, tightened his arms around Aden, and as he sat down drew him onto his knee. Conner and Darric sat on either side of him, just resting their hands on Aden's legs.

"I've worked so hard and for such a long time to make my wolves safe." Blaze smiled and Conner nuzzled his neck. "I thought I was just getting a handle on things, and then you come along."

"And the baby," added Darric in awe.

"I thought we were complete—I was complete, but you just…"

Darric shook his head and Conner interrupted. "It's so hard when you deliberately put yourself in harm's way."

"Constantly," murmured Blaze. He brushed a kiss on Aden's face. "I know you have a job to do as well, a vital one, but—"

"What Blaze is saying." Darric squeezed Aden's leg. "Is that he needs…"

Darric looked helplessly at Conner, and Conner smiled. "A little empathy."

Aden smiled ruefully and shuffled in deeper. Blaze groaned and caught Aden's mouth in his. His smooth tongue demanded all of Aden until he was spinning with sensation. When Blaze captured the back of Aden's head firmly and drew him even nearer, Aden felt the man's possession tug at his insides. He thrust his hips, pushing his cock into that rock hard abdomen.

Aden broke away. "The Senator?"

Conner chuckled. "Everything was going fine until Blaze just stopped mid-sentence and shifted. You should have seen everybody's faces. We just had time to apologize and run after him."

Darric chuckled. "We were showing them the landing sites for the helicopters."

Blaze lifted Aden's chin. "Omega, we have much to do. We haven't fully bonded, and there's the huge issue of starting integration of werewolves into the military."

"The whole mess with your old pack and the doctor," added Darric, "who still hasn't been caught."

Conner bent his head and Aden held his breath in wonder as Conner breathed a soft kiss onto Aden's bare abdomen.

"But the important thing is," Blaze started slowly.

"Is that we're all together," Aden finished for him. He reached out and clasped each of Darric's and Conner's hands, felt Blaze's arms tighten around him. God, he felt so loved, so complete.

Love you, little one.

Okay, thought Aden, smiling. Maybe being called little wasn't always bad.

The End.

Also By

More from Victoria Sue

Shifter Rescue
MM Paranormal MPreg Shifter Romance

First Series
MM MPreg Omegaverse Romance

Hunter's Creek
MM MPreg Shifter Romance

Sirius Wolves Series
MM MPreg Shifter Romance

The Kingdom of Askara
MM Fantasy MPreg Romance

Unexpected Daddies
MM Contemporary Daddy/boy/little

Enhanced World Series
MM Paranormal Urban Fantasy Romance

Heroes and Babies
MM Contemporary Action/Adventure Romance

Guardians of Camelot Series
MM Urban Fantasy Romance

Rainbow Key
MM Contemporary Action/Adventure Romance

Pure
MM BDSM Romance

Innocent Series
MM Historical Romance

Standalones

Love at Frost Bite: Rudy

MM Paranormal Mpreg Romance

Click here to join Victoria's
newsletter to stay up to date on all new releases, special newsletter serials, and exclusive giveaways!

Find Victoria on Social Media

Website

Facebook

Instagram

Made in the USA
Columbia, SC
26 May 2023